ROBERT

Based on a Screenplay written by
Richard Rothstein & Christopher Leitch
and Dean Devlin

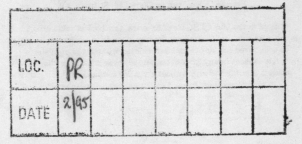

A SIGNET BOOK

SIGNET

Published by the Penguin Group
Penguin Books Ltd, 27 Wrights Lane, London W8 5TZ, England
Penguin Books USA Inc., 375 Hudson Street, New York,
New York 10014, USA
Penguin Books Australia Ltd, Ringwood, Victoria, Australia
Penguin Books Canada Ltd, 10 Alcorn Avenue, Toronto, Ontario,
Canada M4V 3B2
Penguin Books (NZ) Ltd, 182–190 Wairau Road, Auckland 10, New Zealand

Penguin Books Ltd, Registered Offices: Harmondsworth, Middlesex, England

First published in the USA by Jove Books, by arrangement with Carolco
Pictures, Inc., and Carolco International N. V., 1992
First published in Great Britain in Signet 1992
5 7 9 10 8 6 4

Signet Film and TV Tie-in edition published 1992

Prologue

Tsao Li, Vietnam, 1969

The sky over the jungle was a battlefield, a conflict of man and nature. Mortar rounds and tracers struggled for control of the dark night, engaging in a noisy brawl with the rumbling thunder and the bright white lightning. A warm, soaking rain poured into the dense, humid vegetation, turning the clammy jungle floor into a lake of sticky, inky mud.

Witzy, nineteen and more scared than he had ever thought it possible to be, tore through the dense vegetation, beating his way through the bush, slamming his way to safety. The jungle did not cooperate. Lianas, tree limbs, branches seemed to snatch at his clothes like claws, trying to hold him back; the mud was as thick as freshly mixed concrete and strove to suck him down into its clammy depths.

1

The branches lashed across his face, scourging him like a thousand whips, and every few yards the mud would entangle his legs and pitch him headlong into the soupy earth. But he would be up and running again in a second, unmindful of the bruises and cuts, bolting through the jungle, running as if his life depended on escape—because it did.

Suddenly, a hand, a strong human hand, grabbed him from behind and yanked him down, pulling him into a depression in the jungle floor half-filled with water and mud. Witzy felt fear nail him cold, and he shrieked and waited for death.

But there was no hot bullet or cold blade. Instead, Witzy found himself face-to-face with a friend, his platoon leader, Pfc Luc Devreux. Normally Luc would have been a man Witzy trusted his life to—hell, he had done it a thousand times during his tour in 'Nam—but right now Witzy was fleeing a danger that not even Luc could combat.

Luc Devreux looked pretty calm, considering the trouble the whole unit was in, but the two grunts cowering alongside Luc in his makeshift hideout looked about as freaked out as Witzy was.

Witzy struggled in the mud, trying to break free of Luc's grasp. "Let me go!" he hissed, his eyes wide with fear. "We gotta get outta here! Let go of me! They're dead. We gotta get the fuck outta here!"

Luc shoved him back down and threw his

weight on him, grappling with the spooked soldier. "Calm down! We have to stay together or we're dead for sure." Luc was Cajun, from deep in the Louisiana bayou country, and although his family had been in the United States for five generations, he and every one of his relatives spoke with the soft French accent characteristic of his people.

Witzy was in no mood for rational argument. "They're dead. All of them. *Dead*. The whole fucking platoon. Let me go, man. I'm not gonna end up like them." Witzy broke free and took off running through the jungle as if he had the devil on his tail.

Luc and his companions exchanged worried glances. "Shit," said one of the soldiers. "This is very bad shit, very bad . . ." He was edging away from Luc as if he were responsible for the danger all around them.

"I'm getting outta here," said the other soldier. "If the platoon is gone . . ."

"We have to stay together," cautioned Luc.

"Shit on that," said the first soldier and ran, taking off after Witzy.

Luc grabbed the remaining soldier. "We can't just leave them," he said urgently.

"Why the fuck not, man? You heard Witzy. They're *dead*, man. Why the hell should we end up like them?"

"Witzy was so spooked we don't know what's happened to the platoon. He—"

Both men dropped to the ground and took cover

as a mortar round exploded somewhere nearby. The air was suddenly hot with shrapnel and smoke.

"Close enough. I'm getting the fuck outta here."

Luc snatched at his companion's sleeve. "No!"

"Luc," the soldier whispered intensely, as if not wanting to be overheard. "Your tour is almost up. You want to go home in a body bag? Don't be a fool, man, come on. We'll get the fuck outta here together."

"No," said Luc stoutly.

"Your ass, man," said the soldier, following Witzy and the other grunt down the path.

Luc watched him go, waited a moment, then slid a twenty-four-inch bayonet out of its sheath and attached it to the muzzle of his M-16. An M-16A1 5.56mm rifle was not designed to carry a bayonet—rapid-fire weapons rarely had this feature—but Luc was far from the only serviceman who had adapted his rifle to bear a blade. It was almost as if having a basic, visceral weapon, something as simple as two feet of sharp steel, made him more confident, safer.

He hefted the weapon in his hands and started back down the path to find his platoon, hacking his way through the dense jungle as he went.

Tsao Li village was just like any other Vietnamese settlement; the platoon had seen a hundred of them during their time in country. It was the usual makeshift cluster of hooches, a well, an acre or two of rice paddies, some pigsties, chicken coops. The platoon had pulled in that hot morning to the usual welcome: the fearful eyes of the villagers—old women, kids, old men—no one older than eight, no one younger than eighty. The ARVN translator attached to the unit had done his routine, brutal dog-and-pony show. He screamed at the old ladies and slapped the old men around, trying to get someone to admit that they were VC, or they knew who was VC, or they knew where the VC were. As usual, no one knew anything.

Just another day in the beautiful Republic of South Vietnam.

Except it wasn't. There had been an edginess to the morning, a nervous mix of fear and exhaustion, a potent undercurrent of tension.

It was supposed to have been a routine patrol— three days out, followed by three days back at base. They were now in their sixth day on patrol—an extension that had resulted from a series of screw-ups so amateur that Luc half suspected that they had happened by design rather than by accident. Their initial drop had been twenty clicks off the mark, and that meant they had to endure some hard traveling in the jungle just to get in position. They had twice missed resupply from the air—the choppers just hadn't shown up—so rations were low. There were three short-timers in the platoon—Luc one of them—and all three were sure that the Army had arranged this little party just to make their exit from the service that tiny bit more exciting.

By the time they got to Tsao Li, they were a unit rubbed raw. Taking it hardest was Sergeant Andrew Scott. Usually rock solid, Scott had taken the mishaps and discomforts of the last six days personally, cursing his way through the jungle, pissed off and unhappy and not caring who knew about it.

After a while the lieutenant had had the ARVN translator lay off and had announced that the village was cleared, that the citizens of the hamlet of Tsao Li were innocent of any interaction with the Vietcong. Luc had watched Scott closely when he heard the lieutenant's pronouncement. Scott had continued eyeing the villagers malevolently and mumbling darkly about slopes and gooks and how they were all VC . . .

Around midday, the lieutenant had sent Luc and two buck privates out to survey the area around the village, while the rest of the platoon settled down to wait and see if the choppers would be able to find them *this* time.

By nightfall, when it was time to come in, two things had happened. One, the storm, which made it plain that the platoon was not going to get out of the jungle that night, and two, the attack, which made it plain that a lot of soldiers were not going to get out of Vietnam—ever.

It had come out of the thunder, striking like the storm, blowing through Tsao Li and then beyond, farther out in the sector, where another set of poor grunts was at work. Luc and the rest of his unit hadn't even known they were there.

Six or eight hours of confusion later, Luc was making his way back into the quiet village.

A few hours earlier, Tsao Li could not have been mistaken for paradise. Now it looked, quite literally, like hell.

The village had been destroyed, smashed by some kind of explosive fury that had not been content with mere devastation but had tried for annihilation, the total eradication of a hamlet that had never mattered. Oddly, one building at the end of the only street in the village remained standing. There was nothing exceptional about the bamboo hooch. There was no reason that Luc could see for it to be the lone survivor. It was nothing more than another accident of war.

There were burning huts everywhere, blazing vestiges of a poor rural life, and the bodies of the inhabitants lay strewn about like bloody and tattered litter.

With a sudden and electrifying shock, Luc Devreux saw that not all the bodies were those of the hapless villagers of Tsao Li. Here and there were the corpses of American soldiers, members of his own outfit, men he had seen only a few hours earlier . . . They had been dirty, disheveled, generally pissed off about the situation they were in, mightily annoyed at the United States Army—but they had been *alive*. Now they were corpses, anonymous and identical in death. Carcasses.

Luc knelt next to one of the bodies and turned it over, the dead bulk heavy and awkward to manage. The face had been mutilated beyond recognition, slashed in a murderous frenzy. Then he noticed that both ears had been hacked off, slashed from the skull. Quickly he looked around to the other corpses, American and Vietnamese, and saw that they had all been mangled, each stripped of ears.

Luc staggered back, feeling his gorge rise. It was all he could do to stop himself vomiting. He shut his eyes against the grisly vision, fighting the dry heaves, his head spinning.

Then he heard a shot.

His first impulse was to hit the ground, but in the split second between the shot and his reaction, he realized that the bullet hadn't been aimed at him—it hadn't struck him; nor had it kicked up any dirt at his feet. It had been fired a few yards away, inside the only building in the whole hellhole that remained standing.

M-16 at the ready, Luc made his way toward it, his heart pounding and his hands wet with sweat on the stock and trigger. Outside the doorway of the building he paused and listened. From within came nothing but silence and the telltale smell of blow back—a weapon had definitely been fired inside only moments before. He took a deep breath and stepped into the room.

It took a moment for his eyes to become accustomed to the gloom, but he had no trouble recognizing the outlines of cadavers sprawled at his feet. Then, with a jolt he saw three people—three people still alive.

Two of them were children, a boy and a girl, and they were kneeling in the center of the room, their hands tethered behind their backs, bound so tight their bodies seemed to bend them taut, like bowstrings. They looked over their shoulders at Luc, fear in their eyes. They were gagged securely.

The other figure was sitting on the floor of the hut, his back to Luc. Devreux couldn't see his face, but he looked familiar.

"Sarge?" Luc said uncertainly. He half hoped that it wasn't Sergeant Andrew Scott. Luc didn't want to know that a member of his outfit had anything to do with this slaughterhouse.

Devreux and Scott had been friends and had gotten each other out of more tight spots than they cared to remember. Both men were superb soldiers and they had learned from each other, each taking to jungle warfare as if born to it. There was nothing in their backgrounds, though, that suggested that they were natural fighters—Scott was a city kid and Devreux came from the Cajun country of Louisiana—but strength and clear thinking resided in both of them: a combination almost always found in great warriors. But now it seemed that Scott's strength—his mental stamina—had failed him. He had cracked up.

Luc moved a little closer. "Sarge? What the hell happened here?"

Scott didn't answer. He hardly moved, except to raise his hands and tie a leather thong firmly around his neck, knotting it at the back. Then his left hand dropped to a half-empty bottle of scotch.

9

His right hand rested casually on the thick stock of a bowie knife, the tip of the blade embedded in the smooth mud of the hut floor.

He raised the bottle and sloshed down some of the liquor. Then he turned around.

"Christ! Jesus Christ, Sarge!" Luc stumbled back a pace or two.

Hanging around Scott's neck was a string of severed ears, a dozen of them, maybe more, each leaking blood onto his dirty fatigues. In an earthen pot at this feet were more ears floating in a bloody puddle.

Almost as frightening was the look in Scott's eyes. There was a murderous, wild look there, hate and madness blazing out like high beams. He had painted his face too, black ribbons encircling his eyes and blood-red bands on his cheeks and forearms. Luc found it hard to tear his eyes away from the glazed, evil, psychotic look on Scott's face.

"They wouldn't listen," said Scott, his voice low and husky.

The sound seemed to galvanize the two prisoners, the two kids still trussed at Andrew Scott's feet. They started as if pinched and stared hard at Luc, their eyes pleading for help. He could sense their fear like heat from a fire.

"This town was cleared, Sarge," said Luc. "You heard the lieutenant yourself. These people are innocent."

Scott sneered. "Innocent? They're fucking traitors. You turn around and they stab you in the back."

"But what about the others? Your own men? They wouldn't stab you in the back."

"What the hell does a farm boy like you know about war? You can't trust anybody. Never. Do you understand me?"

Luc sighed heavily. There was no point in arguing with Scott—he had wigged out so bad that there was no chance of ever bringing him back from craziness. Now all Luc could think about was getting out of there alive.

"Hey, Sarge, my tour is just about up. I'm short. I just want to go home."

This simple suggestion seemed to annoy Scott more than the treachery of Vietnamese villagers. "You're just like all the others," he snarled. "You just want to leave. Like none of this shit ever happened. Listen to me, farm boy, it happened. Got it? It happened!" He advanced a step or two, the bowie knife glittering in his hand. "You can't just walk away! It doesn't just go away! You hear me?"

"I hear you, Sarge," Luc whispered, edging toward the door.

"Do you *hear* me?!" Scott screamed and threw himself at Luc, the bowie knife arcing in the gloom, coming to rest on the edge of Devreux's ear, ready to slice.

"You're just a traitor too, aren't you, farm boy? That's all you fuckin' grunts are." Scott was leaning in, whispering into the ear he was on the verge of shaving from Luc's skull. "Another fuckin' traitor, that's all you are, right?"

Luc managed to shake his head, feeling the edge of the blade on his skin. "No," he whispered, "I'm no traitor, Sarge."

Scott smiled. "No? Then prove it." He shoved Luc's own rifle into his hands and pointed at the little girl. "Prove it by killing her. Kill this motherfucking little traitor."

Tears were streaming down the face of the little girl.

Luc was frozen, unable to move a muscle. He looked from the girl back to Scott.

"Kill her. That's an order."

Luc shook his head. "I can't."

"Shit," said Scott. "It's easy." He slid a pistol out of the holster on his hip and raised the heavy weapon, aiming at the girl's head.

The boy screamed behind his gag and threw himself to the side, knocking the girl from the line of fire.

"No!" screamed Luc.

The bullet smacked into the center of the boy's forehead, opening an ugly red wound, then blew out the back of his head in a hideous mess of bone and hair.

Scott, completely unmoved by this ghastly sight, drew a bead on his next victim, swiveling his gun hand toward the girl, ready to kill again.

Luc reacted, hardly aware of what he was doing. He slammed the butt of his rifle into Andrew Scott's head, throwing him back into the gloomy recesses of the hut. Devreux grabbed the girl by the shoulder and shoved her toward the door.

"Run!"

Together they dashed out of the shack and into the night, propelled by fear and the desire for survival. The fires still burned, lighting the night and throwing a ghoulish glow onto the bodies scattered in the street.

A bullet hummed past Luc's ear. He shot a glance over his shoulder and saw Scott standing in the doorway of the hooch, a jagged gash from Luc's gun bleeding on the sergeant's brow. The pistol bucked in Scott's hand, a second shot, and a flash later Luc felt the hot bullet burrow into his thigh. There was no pain—not yet—just a numbness, like a hard punch.

Luc pitched forward into the dirt, his rifle flying from his hands. A wave of nausea and dizziness broke over him as his body finally registered the damage that had been done to it. The Vietnamese girl dashed on ahead, running for her life.

With Luc Devreux downed and immobile, Scott turned his attention to the girl. He unclipped a grenade from the ammo belt at his waist and ran past Luc, then stopped and set, like a pitcher about to fire a short, sharp fastball.

Luc watched in horror. "Sarge! No! *Please* . . ."

The pin clicked out of the grenade, and Scott hurled the bomb at the girl, who had almost reached the safety of the underbrush that encircled the village. It fell at her feet and detonated. There was a flash and an explosion, and the girl simply disappeared, the shards of hot metal scything her thin body into a hundred pieces.

Scott turned from the carnage he had made and stepped into the mean, hard blade of Luc's bayonet. Something in the horrible and pointless death of a nameless Vietnamese girl had given Devreux the strength to overcome his pain, retrieve his rifle and get Scott and get him good. It never occurred to him to shoot the sergeant—something animal in him took over, something that made him want to make Scott's end as brutal and as bloody as the death of the girl.

The steel was embedded in Scott's chest—Luc could feel the skewered body alive and pulsing along the shaft of the blade—and the sergeant's eyes grew wide and disbelieving, staring at his former comrade, as if not quite able to credit him with his bloody and savage demise.

Then, he managed one more act in his brutal life. Scott raised his pistol and fired, a bullet punching into Luc's chest. The force of the point-blank shot tossed him back, pulling the bayonet out of Scott. But Luc's finger was curled around the trigger of his weapon, and he loosed a quick rip of bullets as he fell, the slugs chewing up Scott's body.

Both men dropped to the ground, their shattered bodies joining the others scattered there, two final touches on a horrific tableau.

The choppers showed up the next morning, and it didn't take long for the resupply team to figure out that something had gone very, very wrong at Tsao Li. Within the hour there were two more helicopters on the site, one from Graves Registration, the other without unit markings. The GR chopper disgorged a team, which set about assembling the American corpses and packing them in vinyl body bags. These were laid out as neat as a cord of wood. The other machine had a single passenger, a spit-and-polish-officer in perfect fatigues, who surveyed the scene before him, shocked, yet grim faced.

All the cadavers had been packed in body bags and the GR guys were reading off the tags. One dug in the bag for the ID discs while the other noted the name on a form mounted on a clipboard. The officer watched them go about their bleak business.

When they got to the bag containing the remains of Scott, the soldier had to root around in the sack like a kid at a grab bag.

"No tags?" asked the guy with the clipboard.

He unzipped the bag and reached farther in. "Can't find the tag . . . What the hell happened here?" His hand closed around something and pulled it out.

It took a second for the nature of his find to sink in. "Jesus Christ!" Scared to death and sick to his stomach he flung away the chain of ears that had decorated Scott's chest.

"Fuck it!" said his companion. "I thought the VC did that. Not one of our own guys."

"Now we know where all the ears went."

The officer had come over and was staring at Scott's body, staring hard, the way a farmer appraises livestock. He shook his head, nodding to himself.

"I'd hate to be the poor schmuck who has to explain this shit to ma and pa back home," said the guy who had found the chair of ears.

"How're we supposed to write this up? What do we say happened here?" asked the soldier with the clipboard.

"Nothing," said the captain shortly. "Nothing happened here at all. MIA. We didn't find anyone. Do you understand me?"

It was completely against the book, but the two GR guys were pfcs and the captain was a captain. If that was the way the captain wanted it, that was the way he was going to get it.

"Yessir," they said, in unison.

The officer strode over to the company radio, took the headphones off the operator and slipped them on. He changed the frequency on the radio set, stepping up a channel, and then started transmitting. "Lincoln, this is Eagle," he said into the receiver. "Come in . . ."

The radioman didn't much care for the treatment he had just received, but like the GR soldiers, he knew that a captain was a captain.

Lincoln, whoever he might be, had answered the call. "I've got a code Zebra, do you copy?" announced the captain. Then he listened a moment. "Only a few hours ago. At least ten bodies, maybe more. Yes sir . . . Eagle out." He handed the phones back to the radio operator.

"Pack the bodies in ice," he told the Graves Registration workers. "Fast."

The two men exchanged glances. "Ice, sir?"

"That's right. You have ice in your chopper, don't you?" The captain knew that it was standard equipment for a Graves Registration unit.

"Yes sir, we got ice."

"Then pack 'em."

"All of 'em?"

"That's what I said, soldier."

"Okay, sir." The two guys knelt down and zipped closed the two bags nearest to them. First Scott, then Luc.

Chapter One

The Nevada Desert, The Present Day

The giant cargo plane slipped out of the blue sky over the Nevada desert. The aircraft, a C-130, the old workhorse of the Air Force, one of the toughest and most versatile planes in the entire inventory, touched down on the tarmac of the desert strip, the wheels squealing on the hot asphalt. The airstrip was an old one, and, these days, if it was used at all, it was as a junking ground for old, out-of-date and decommissioned aircraft. The hulks of eighteen or twenty antiquated planes lay scattered around the perimeter of the field, slowly rusting down to nothing but dust, like the bones of dinosaurs.

Almost as soon as the wheels of the C-130 hit, six army Jeeps maneuvered through the barrier of dead ships and raced out toward the giant aircraft, surrounding the machine and escorting it as it taxied in. The Jeeps, each with a .50-caliber machine gun mounted on the bed behind, looked like puny bodyguards encircling the heavyweight champ.

Standing on the edge of the tarmac was a lone army colonel. He watched the plane intently through his RayBans, then checked his watch. The C-130 was ninety seconds late and that annoyed him.

"Get a move on!" he yelled, his voice lost in the roar of the four engines that drove the props.

Colonel Worth Perry was the kind of man who took ninety seconds' worth of tardiness very seriously. He was tall and well built, as tough and as mean as a whip; he didn't like it when things did not go strictly according to plan. But, as a lifelong Special Forces officer, he knew that things did not adhere to meticulous timetables and he could be flexible—he had to be; it was something that was built into the job he had to do. He was already thinking of ways to get those ninety seconds back—how could he push his unit a little harder to make up for lost time?

Even before the enormous plane had rolled to a halt on the hardstand, fatigue-clad technicians were swarming over the aircraft, making ready to open the nose-cone loading-bay door. They slid ramps up to the lip of the plane and then stood back. From within the guts of the ship came the sound of a powerful diesel engine bursting into life, and a second later a giant eighteen-wheel tractor-trailer truck roared out of the plane and raced down the ramps onto the runway hard-stand.

It was a very mean-looking vehicle. Roughly thirty-five feet long, the truck was as solid and as square as a railway locomotive and paneled in dark green olive-drab steel armor plating. It bristled with antennae and had two small satellite dishes angled on the roof. Three small radar wings revolved quickly in housings along the side of the vehicle, and every ten feet a small video camera swept back and forth, its electronic eye scanning the area around the truck.

There were 7.62mm automatic machine guns mounted on the armored cab, on the sides and at the rear. These were unmanned. At a press of the button in the control cockpit these two self-operating weapons would open up, spewing out fifty-four hundred rounds a minute, creating around the vehicle a killing zone destined to annihilate anyone unlucky enough to venture too close without permission.

The truck halted on the tarmac, and the loud hum of hydraulic machinery began eminating from deep within the deadly-looking vehicle. Giant though it already was, as the hydraulic equipment kicked in, the truck began to expand, as steel extensions grew out of its walls, enlarging the trailer some nine meters on all sides.

The few soldiers on the ground who had never seen the Unisol Command and Transport Center before could only watch awestruck. Within the traveling behemoth, there was no time to marvel

21

at the machine. Inside, it was all business as usual.

White-coated technicians worked in the core of the truck, sitting hunched over a dizzying array of dials and monitor screens.

Woodward Haines, the chief technician in the tracking device room of the Unisol Truck, leaned in close to study a scroll of figures and stats flashing on his screen. Everything was in order.

"Okay," he said, "let's fire 'em up."

"Got it," said Garth, his younger colleague. He punched a series of buttons and then peered at his monitor.

The screen crackled to life, showing a section in another part of the huge truck. It was the Unisol laboratory and cooling chamber, the heart of the whole vehicle. The air in there was frigid, as in a mammoth refrigerator, and like a freezer, it stored meat. In the glass-encased room stood a row of naked men, big like sides of beef in a meat locker. They were massive individuals, broad-shouldered and pumped up, with bulging muscles and sinews like steel cables.

For a long moment they stood stock-still, inert and seemingly dead in the icy chamber. As Garth transmitted instructions to the cooling room, the bodies began to move, slowly at first and then faster, like zombies coming to consciousness at the mumblings of a voodoo high priest.

In a matter of seconds, they were a blur of motion. Two bulky lockers were dragged open, and the men began donning their uniforms, dressing themselves as if they were knights putting on their armor. Armored chest plates were snapped in place, heavy brown boots were laced tight, weighty harnesses festooned with lethal-looking gear were slipped over broad shoulders and locked into position. One by one, the men lined up and marched to the exit of the chamber.

Garth was waiting for them outside the truck. The airfield was a wild swarm of action now. A helicopter was sitting by the truck, its rotors whirling, its engines howling. A jeep was streaking across the tarmac, carrying Colonel Perry and his aide, a lieutenant named Sullivan.

The first soldier stepped up to Garth. The technician fussed over the details of the man's uniform, fitting him with an elaborate high-tech piece of headgear. It looked like a micro-sized video cam corder, the viewfinder fitting neatly over the soldier's left eye. A wire-thin microphone sprouted from the apparatus, curling down to the lips of the trooper.

Garth watched as the eyepiece of the video camera rotated, focusing itself and settling on his face. He grinned into the lens, like a tourist having his picture taken.

"How's the picture?"

Woodward Haines, in the Unisol truck control, "seeing" through the soldier's eyes, laughed. "Pretty ugly."

The next soldier presented himself for inspection, a black guy of bruising size. Garth quickly looked him over, fitted him with his gear and then sent him on his way.

Colonel Perry's Jeep had pulled up next to the truck. He checked his watch, still fretting about those lost ninety seconds.

"Get a move on," he yelled, striving to make himself heard above the storm of the helicopter engines. "We don't have much time."

"Yessir!"

The next soldier strode into place. It was Luc Devreux. He was the same age he had been in 1969; he looked as he had always looked—and yet, different. His handsome face had a hardened, emotionless expression, like an automaton brought to life in some mad doctor's mountain lab. Next up was Andrew Scott—unaged, unemotional, hard, tough looking, robotic, but nonetheless a human being, alive.

Assembled on the tarmac, the Universal Soldiers were an awesome, rather terrifying sight. There were a dozen of them, each a broad shouldered, strong, stony looking man. Their bulging muscles were encased in desert camouflage body armor, their legs crisscrossed with belts strapping various pieces of equipment to their bodies. Buckled to each wrist was an elaborate chronometer, a maze of dials that also gave readings of pulse, body temperature, blood pressure and heart rate. Lashed to their broad backs were small water- and flameproof duffel bags of the same design as their uniforms. Two of the team were black, one Asian.

They did not wear a lot in the way of insignia.

24

On each of their left sleeves, on the upper arm, was the spearhead and the designation "Special Forces"; on the right sleeve, the skull and crossbones of a sniper. Across their hearts a tape read simply, "US Army" and above that were the small gold wings of the paratroops and airborne. On the left side of each man's chest was a small American flag patch and a tape that read, "USSF—United States Special Forces."

Their primary weapon was a submachine gun, a deadly Heckler and Koch MP5A3 nine-millimeter. The weapons were just over a foot long, but packed into those few inches of steel was an astounding amount of firepower. The rate of fire from the lethal guns was blindingly fast, and they carried the option of converting to grenade launchers. The MP5A3 was also deadly accurate—it had little back kick and practically no forward moving mass—and in experienced hands it was a vicious weapon. The Universal Soldiers looked as if they had all the experience necessary to use the submachine guns to the limit of their efficiency.

None of the soldiers smiled—they didn't even look nervous. They seemed to be completely without emotion, human machines dedicated to one task: killing.

"Okay," yelled Colonel Perry. "Move out."

As one, the Universal Soldiers took off running toward the helicopter, throwing themselves into the cargo bay. In a matter of seconds, the chopper was loaded and on its way racing low over the desert, then into the gorge of the Colorado River.

The pilot was as good at his job as the soldiers were at theirs. He kept the machine down, well below the level of the summit of the gorge itself, using the shelter as protection, as if he expected to come under attack at any moment.

The helicopter followed the river as if it was on a highway in the air, then banked sharply left and gained altitude, zooming over the lifeless mountains and the harsh landscape on the slopes. Once over that rocky hurdle, the chopper dropped down again, and in a moment a glimpse of a dam, the immense McKinley Dam, flashed into view. The chopper was way down low now, the skids almost touching the water, coming straight at the dam on the downriver side. Then, abruptly, the craft soared over the towering dam, giving the soldiers a brief glimpse of the top of the barrier.

On the crest of the dam sat a squat, blockhouse-like structure with a single window looking downstream. Beneath it were double metal doors. It was the terminus of the elevator that ran deep into the bowels of the dam, connecting the top with the power station that was crouched at the base of the structure, on the upriver side. It was not, normally, a remarkable thing to look at. Except—today the passengers in the chopper could see very clearly in the bright sunshine that a number of bodies lay sprawled at the foot of the elevator building. Blood pooled around them, puddles of gore on the warm concrete. There were five of them—not soldiers or even criminals. They were tourists, innocent bystanders.

The chopper swept by, overshooting the dam by a mile and a half, and then dropped rapidly toward the rocky shore.

Back at the Unisol command truck, Woodward and Garth had been tracking its progress. As it neared the staging point, Woodward nodded to himself and started issuing orders.

"Begin cutoff."

Garth caught his cue. He leaned into the microphone on the console in front of him. "Okay, boys, pack 'em away."

The helicopter was hovering now, just a few yards above the river, the blades of the rotor churning up the water. Inside, the Unisols methodically removed their headsets and stowed them in their duffel bags. That done, they began to drop, one by one, from the chopper into the raging waters below.

The images on the monitors in the command truck fizzled and then vanished in a cloud of static. Garth turned to Woodward.

"Communications severed," he reported. "We're out of contact for the next six minutes."

"Now we wait," said Woodward.

High in the craggy hills that looked down on the dam, concealed among the rocks and crevasses, were members of the local police SWAT team, the first people to respond to the sketchy reports that something bloody had happened at the summit of the McKinley Dam. They were armed with high-powered sniper's rifles, the British Enfield L42A1—

7.62mm, accurate to a range of twenty-five hundred yards—and they were itching to use them.

The sharpshooters had been on the scene for almost twenty minutes, watching a grisly hostage situation unfold before their eyes—a predicament they were totally powerless to terminate. They were reduced to being forward observers, reporting the action on the dam back to a command post nearby staffed with more local cops, a swarm of FBI agents and Colonel Perry.

The SWAT team member closest to the dam was still so far away that he had to watch the events through the scope of his rifle. He had the elevator doors squarely in the cross hairs of his sight when they swept open, exposing a hostage, his hands behind his head.

"They're bringing the next one out." Although he was almost a thousand yards away, the sharpshooter whispered the information into his microphone, as if he didn't want to spook the gunman or his captive.

The tourist stepped out of the elevator, blinking in the bright light. Then he caught sight of the bodies scattered at the mouth of the elevator and froze in terror.

"We got one bad guy inside the elevator," reported the SWAT cop. He had the cross hairs squarely on the chest of the gunman and his finger inched on the trigger. "Requesting green light."

At the command post the ranking police officer, an FBI special field agent named Winston, seized the microphone. "Negative! Do you read me? We can't take one of them down. They're all linked together over a communications system. One goes and all hell breaks loose. You got that?"

The sharpshooter got it—the same time the hostage got it. There was a single shot from inside the elevator, and a slug slammed into the prisoner's head. The shot echoed off the hills and rolled down the valley, a small peel of thunder. The hostage tumbled into the heap of his fellow victims.

In the command post they heard the SWAT cop breathe into his microphone. "Jesus Christ . . ."

"Never mind him," said Perry. "Do you see my guys?"

The sharpshooter pulled himself together and swiveled the barrel of his rifle upstream from the dam. "Yeah, we have a splashdown." He could just make out the Unisols swimming fast through the water, though they hardly made a ripple. They were headed toward the two tall intake towers of the power station like a school of sharks. "They're in the water."

"How far?" demanded Perry.

"'Bout a mile and a half."

"A mile and a half!" The chief cop, Winston, was really worried now. "Your guys are a mile and a half away?" He glanced at his watch. "Perry, we've only got thirteen minutes before they bring out the next hostage. They'll never make it."

Perry didn't seem to be concerned at all about time. They had gotten those errant ninety seconds back. Everything was on schedule; the Unisols were performing to specifications.

"Relax," said Colonel Perry soothingly. "Plenty of time. Just one question . . ."

"What's that?"

"Can someone get me a cup of coffee?"

Chapter Two

Veronica Roberts pushed the gas pedal of her Wagoneer to the floor, and the heavy vehicle chewed up the desert road, racing toward the McKinley Dam. She took one hand off the wheel and fiddled with the radio, tuning it to an all-news station and turning the volume up loud. The broadcast was not coming live from the site, but being read from a news-wire. The station was in far-off Reno, and the communiqué was broken up every few seconds by the crackle of static.

She fumbled for her notebook, and without her eyes leaving the road in front of her, she started scribbling, cribbing the story she would have to report in a few minutes time from the radio station summary. It wasn't exactly ethical, but right then Veronica Roberts didn't have time for ethics.

". . . with thirty hostages held inside the base of the power station, the situation remains unclear at this time. Using the hostages as human shields, the gunmen have made a variety of demands, including the immediate release of the seven of their comrades accused in the bombing of—" The announcer's voice was lost to a blizzard of static.

"Bombing of what?" Veronica yelled at the radio. "What the hell did they bomb?"

The interference cleared. "—in Frankfurt, Germany, late last year."

"Got it, " said Veronica to herself. She was a reporter and a good one, and in her head she kept meticulous files of recent disasters, catastrophes, mishaps and murders. There had been a terrorist bombing of a NATO facility in Germany the year before. A number of the perpetrators were nabbed by German police and security forces before the bad guys got out of the country. A radical splinter group had vowed revenge, and this outrage on the McKinley Dam, half a world away from Central Europe, was the result.

Veronica felt better—she had some kind of handle on the story now, so she rewarded herself, shoveling a cigarette into her mouth and lighting it with the electric lighter set in the dashboard. She exhaled. Now her only problem was getting to her broadcast crew to do a live remote. She was very, very late and the satellite had been booked. If she made it, she would be a hero. If she didn't, she would probably be unemployed.

"Shitshitshit," she hissed through clenched

teeth. Ahead of her on the highway was a police roadblock. She screeched to a halt.

A heavy state trooper, Smokey-the-Bear hat and all, leaned into the cab. "Dam's closed, lady."

"I'm press," she yelled, almost jamming her press pass in his sweaty red face. She gunned the engine and left the cop standing in the dust.

A few hundred yards up the road all was pandemonium. There were dozens of police cars, military vehicles, ambulances and, she was chagrined to see, broadcast trucks from the competition—the three networks and CNN. The van from her own network, Cable News of America, was parked in the thick of it, and she could see her boss and her crew standing around and pacing nervously. A cordon of police stood between the press and the command post where Perry was following the happenings on the dam.

Roberts quickly checked her makeup in the mirror, then jumped out of the truck, stuffing her notes into the pocket of her CNA blazer.

Charles Hoover, her field producer, was furious when she ran up to him. "Where the hell have you been? I was just about to cancel the remote."

"Keep your shirt on, Charles. I'm here, aren't I? You knew I'd make it. Never had any doubts, right? I'm just running a little late, that's all."

"A little!" said Charles indignantly. "You're on in—how long, Huey?"

"Fifteen seconds. You're on the air in fifteen, " said Huey. He handed her a microphone and then retreated behind the camera, training the lens on her face.

"Plenty of time."

"Where the hell were you?" demanded Charles. "I've been calling your hotel for hours." He was standing just outside of camera range. If he was worried about upsetting his correspondent just before she went on live, he didn't show it.

Veronica was assuming her "network face" and didn't bother to look over at her apoplectic producer. "Ever hear about getting a lead, Charles? Tell me if you don't understand any of these technical terms . . ."

"Eight, seven, six—" Huey counted off.

"Where the hell are your notes?" yelled Charles.

For a split second, Veronica panicked—then she remembered and dug her few tattered notes from her blazer pocket.

"Four, three, two—" droned Huey.

"Veronica! Cigarette!"

Veronica spat the cigarette out of her mouth.

"And one—" Huey gave the "you're on" signal, and Veronica's image appeared on TV screens all over the United States.

The people watching the broadcast would never have been able to guess of the turmoil that had enveloped Veronica and her crew in the seconds leading up to the transmission. She seemed calm and collected, completely in control of the situation, giving a measured and unhysterical account of the events at the dam. She recounted the facts as she knew them: thirty hostages were being held—including a group of Japanese tourists on a sightseeing tour of the Far West—and the number of casualties so far. She listed the terrorists' demands and the lack of a response from the government. She proved once again that she was what she said she was: a smart, highly competent newsperson with the ability to think on her feet. She looked cool and composed, gravely concerned by the gruesome story she was bringing into American living rooms.

The report lasted about three minutes, the control room at network headquarters shifting from Veronica to footage of the dam shot earlier in the day. They returned to Veronica, though, for the sign-off.

". . . from the McKinley Dam, this is Veronica Roberts reporting live for CNA."

"And we're out," said Huey.

All three of them sighed heavily. Veronica immediately started looking for a cigarette. She needed to relax, to catch her breath.

Charles, however, was not about to let her off the hook. He was still mightily angry at her. "Veronica—"

She was just lighting up. "See," she said with a little smirk, "I told you there would be no problem."

"No problem! In case you haven't noticed, this network does *not* revolve around you."

Veronica feigned elaborate surprise, as if she had just been hit with a major bombshell. "You mean to tell me I'm *not* the center of the universe?"

"Don't crack wise with me, Veronica."

It was time for a little conciliation. "Come on, Charles, lighten up a little. Okay, I don't play by your rules, but I always get you the story."

"Yeah, well, I'm sick of this goddam prima donna attitude of yours. You think that because you broke a few stories in your career that you're indispensable? Think again."

"Come on, Charles. What the hell is that supposed to mean?"

"It means—you're fired!"

"What, *Chuck*?"

"You heard me." Charles folded his arms across his chest like a bouncer with instructions to keep an undesirable off the premises.

"Fire me? You don't have the authority to fire me. You're a field producer, for God's sake. I'm talent."

"Not anymore," Charles shot back. "I had a little chat with the network this morning, Ronnie, and they agree with me. You're out. Thank God!" He turned on his heel and marched away.

Veronica Roberts's blue eyes were blazing in anger. "You can't do that!" she yelled after her former producer. She turned to Huey, who was packing up the equipment, just keeping his head down.

"Can they do that?" she demanded.

Huey shrugged. "Well," he said, "they just did, didn't they?"

"But I'm in the union!" she hollered in outrage.

While Veronica Roberts's personal drama was unfolding in the press area next to the dam, a more deadly drama was about to unfold within the dam itself.

Luc and Scott, leaders of the Universal Soldiers team—or, to give them their Unisol designations, GR 44 and GR 13—had reached the base of the dam, right at the power station. Treading water, they stared up at the giant building looming above them, paying special attention to the tall intake towers.

The barrels of their MP5A3 submachine guns broke the surface of the water, each weapon fitted with the grenade-launching attachment—but instead of a grenade, the guns were loaded with grappling hooks attached to long lengths of cord. It was not ordinary rope, but extremely lightweight line, as tough and as strong as steel cable, with only a quarter of the poundage.

They fired in unison, the grappling hooks soaring up the towers and locking on the uppermost lip. Luc Devreux and Andrew Scott tested their weight against the line, then hauled themselves out of the water, climbing the towers effortlessly, hand over hand.

The moment they emerged from the choppy flow they were spotted by the sharpshooter. He blinked as they climbed the towers, not quite able to believe his eyes: the soldiers were racing up the sides of the buildings, their powerful arms and legs working like pistons.

"I see them," he said into the headset of his radio. "And they are hauling ass."

Now it was Winston's turn to be startled. He studied his watch. "They covered a mile and a half, in the water, in under four minutes?" he asked Perry incredulously.

Colonel Perry checked his own timepiece and grimaced. "They're eight seconds behind schedule."

The SWAT sharpshooter's voice crackled over the radio. "They've reached the top of the towers and they're heading across the catwalks that connect 'em to the top of the dam." They had made a one-hundred-foot climb in about forty seconds. "Just who the hell *are* these guys?"

From the top of the dam, Luc and Andrew could look down the exposed exterior shaft of the elevator. At each level stood a single gunman, a communication helmet on his head, a black mask obliterating his features, his weapon at the ready.

Silently, the two Unisols opened their duffels and put on their headsets. Back at the Universal Soldier command truck, stationed miles away at the desert airstrip, the monitors burst back into life, confused screens full of static and snow.

Garth jumped as if he had been given an electric shock. "We're back on!"

"Get busy," ordered Woodward. "Clear that image. And prepare for record."

"Got it," said Garth, almost diving for the controls of the monitors. He fine-tuned the focus on the Unisols' headsets and set the sensitive tape recorders in the unit to pick up every sound above a whisper and reproduce it perfectly.

On the dam, Luc Devreux and Scott caught the words the thugs spoke into their headsets. It was the regularly scheduled two-minute check-in that the gunmen had been making continuously during the long hour since the hostage drama began.

"Checkpoint one, all clear."

"Checkpoint two, all clear."

The Unisols were ready to strike the first blow against the terrorists. Each man fitted a short silencer into the barrel of his Heckler and Koch and took aim on the two gunmen on the uppermost level.

They fired simultaneously, the deadly little weapons emitting a sound hardly louder than a cough. The effects, however, were devastating. Bullets slammed into the heads of the gunmen, dropping them, silent and dead, to the metal floor.

In the Universal Soldier command truck Garth saw the bullets strike home and shook his fist in the air, like a football fan whose team had just scored.

"Awright! Wicked!"

The chief technician was more businesslike. "Interceptors are secured and powered, " droned Woodward. "Stand by to begin playback."

"Standing by," said Garth.

Woodward was watching his stopwatch. At the two-minute mark he cued Garth, who hit the controls. "Checkpoint one, all clear," said the late gunman's gravelly voice.

"Checkpoint two, " said his deceased colleague, "all clear."

Deep down in the bowels of the power station, the terrorist commander, Wagner, and his associates heard the reports and did not suspect for a second that something was seriously amiss with their lookouts.

Garth turned to Woodward and high-fived him. The hastily concocted plan seemed to be working. "They swallowed it whole," he said.

Woodward agreed. "They seem to be buying it. Time for the next phase . . ."

Luc Devreux and Andrew Scott began rapelling down the side of the dam, sliding down the ropes at incredible speed, the ropes hot in their gloved hands.

They hit the landing of the power station, dropping noiselessly behind two terrorist snipers guarding the rear entrance to the generating depot.

With a vicious kick, Luc slammed his foot into the neck of one of the goons, snapping his spine like a wishbone. Scott had his prey in a powerful choke hold, silently crushing the network of bones and cartilage in his neck, quickly, deftly, squeezing the life out of the man. Luc dispatched his victim efficiently. Scott seemed to relish the manner of death he was inflicting.

Back in the Unisol truck Garth winced at the amplified sound of bones cracking. "I'm getting the feeling he's starting to like this shit."

"Don't be ridiculous," Woodward snapped. "He doesn't know how to like. Just do your job and let him do his."

"Right," said Garth.

The rest of the Unisol team were joining up with the two advance men, swimming up out of the black water and clambering onto the power station landing, their guns, fitted with silencers now, at the ready. The moment they hit dry land, they unzipped their bags and clamped on their headgear. No one spoke; no one looked even mildly apprehensive, let alone scared or fearful.

One of the Unisols, one of the black guys, designated GR 74, had an extra piece of equipment—a pair of ordinary gray denim overalls, the best disguise the Universal Soldiers command could come up with on short notice. He squeezed himself into the garment, tucking a Colt .45 automatic into the deep pocket that ran down his pants leg. GR 74 did not put his communications gear on his head as the others had done. Instead, he fastened it to the top of a workman's metal toolbox. If you didn't look too closely at the man, you might have mistaken him for a worker at the power station who had, by accident, stumbled into the bloody events at McKinley Dam.

Andrew Scott and Luc Devreux took a moment to count bodies, making sure that their force was intact and unimpaired, then guided their small detachment into the tunnels that ran back into the dark depths of the dam itself.

They moved silently, swiftly, unchallenged in the murky shaft, stopping only when they reached the first set of metal doors. Here the crew stopped and crouched. Luc gestured GR 74 forward, motioning him through the door. GR 74 nodded and advanced, walking straight into the nest of terrorists in the power station control room.

It was becoming apparent to Wagner, the leader of the terrorists, that he was going to have to kill a few more hostages, and if that didn't get the attention of the authorities, he was going to destroy the dam itself. His team of gunmen had laid explosives in strategic points throughout the structure, ready to be detonated by remote control from the sophisticated communications briefcase he had set up in the control room. But before deciding to blow himself and his team to kingdom come, there was the matter of which captive would die next.

They were all lined up there in the command center, eleven people bound, gagged and on their knees, waiting under the watchful eyes of three heavily armed gunmen.

Wagner glanced at his watch. "I think it's time . . . ," he said ominously. He ran his eyes over the rank of his terrified prisoners, like a diner looking over a menu.

Before he could choose his next victim, GR 74 walked into the control room, toolbox in hand. His stolid features were set firmly, totally unaware, it seemed, of the incredible danger he was about to confront.

For a second or two, Wagner and his gunmen could only stare at the figure walking toward them. None of them noticed the camera on the toolbox, which was reading the chamber and feeding information back to the Universal Soldier command truck and directly into a computer, which deciphered the information instantaneously and sent it back to Garth for transmission. The computer was also programmed to distinguish between the terrorists and the hostages, but you didn't need a computer to tell them apart.

Garth whispered into his microphone, sending his voice directly to a tiny receiver, no bigger than a hearing aid, plugged into GR 74's ear.

"Okay," said Garth, "listen up, big guy. You got two gunmen, armed with semi-automatics, fully loaded. They are at twenty-six and thirty-nine degrees respective." Wagner's astonished face filled Garth's monitor. "We got the main target to the rear, he's got a pistol, loaded, and an explosives detonator in the briefcase. When you hit him, hit him clean . . ."

GR 74 nodded. He was still coming, walking straight toward Wagner.

"Who the fuck are you?" The gunman between GR 74 and Wagner advanced on him, his weapon leveled at the Unisol's chest. "Stop! Hold it right there!"

GR 74 didn't seem to have heard.

"I said stop!"

"Shoot him," ordered Wagner.

That was all they needed. The gunmen opened up, bullets blasting in the room, slamming into GR 74's body. GR 74 was rocked off his feet, big slugs ripping into his chest, his body jolted violently. The Unisol swayed on his feet for a moment, then toppled to the floor, falling heavily, like a statue pulled off its pedestal.

Finally, the firing stopped. GR 74 seemed to have walked straight into a hot wave of bullets, impervious to the dangers, a move as suicidal as the taking of the dam itself. The hostages were now frightened beyond their known limits of fear, and they peered out, petrified, from the cover they had taken hastily when the shooting began. But the gunmen were spooked too, not quite able to believe that someone could walk into such fire without flinching.

"What the hell was that?" asked one of them.

"It could be a trap," said Wagner nervously. "Check him out. Do it!"

The two gunmen scurried over to the fallen Unisol and stared hard at the corpse. There was blood and tissue everywhere. It was not a pretty sight.

"He's long gone," said one of them.

"Dead," said the other.

"Check out the corridor," ordered Wagner.

They stepped out into the hall and peered left and right and saw nothing. The minute the two thugs turned their backs, however, GR 74 sat bolt upright, the heavy Colt revolver already in his hand. He fired one shot, the bullet slapping dead center in Wagner's forehead.

At the sound of the blast, the two terrorists turned in time to face Scott and Luc, who had dropped through the maintenance vents in the ceiling of the room. The two Unisols opened up and cut the two astonished gunmen down with three clean shots to the heart.

They turned and swept the room with their weapons, looking for more targets. There were none. The hostages were screaming, crying, fainting in fear. GR 74 sat quietly, holding his guts in with his hands.

Garth's voice came through Andrew Scott's headpiece. "GR 13—status report?"

"GR 13. Arizona team, all clear." Scott's voice was clipped and businesslike.

"Remaining hostages all accounted for? No further injuries."

"Correct," said Scott.

"Nevada team status report?"

Luc—Nevada team leader—didn't respond. He was staring at the rank of Japanese tourists, the hostages kneeling in a corner of the room. Suddenly a nerve in his chiseled cheek began to twitch. Somewhere in the depths of his brain a signal flashed. Two of the Japanese tourists were children, a boy and a girl. They were tethered tightly and crying.

Suddenly, Luc smelled the hot smoke of battle and the cold smell of blood, the humid odor of fear, sweat and desperation. There were sounds too, the crash and rumble of battle, sounds he knew he had heard once but couldn't remember where or when.

"Nevada team report," said Garth.

The girl was crying piteously, and gradually the strains of her sobs and wails mixed and fused with the same sounds from long ago.

"GR 44? Report?"

Luc felt an overpowering confusion, a bewilderment that did not set well with his routine of giving and taking orders.

"GR 44? Do you read?" Garth was getting worried now. He upped his volume. "Report, GR 44."

"There are problems with the equipment?" asked Woodward. It wasn't clear if he was talking about the transmitter or the man himself.

"The system is fine," said Garth, puzzled. "*He's* not responding."

Woodward leaned into the microphone mounted on his command console. "GR 44, status report. Now!"

But Luc was not hearing their voices. Instead, he was listening to another voice, one that seemed familiar, but he couldn't place it. A voice lost somewhere in time.

But the voice was clear: " . . . The town was cleared, Sarge." The voice was young and scared but known to him. "These people are innocent . . ."

Then there was another voice, also known to

him. The voice was harsh, vehement, wild and deranged. "They're fucking traitors . . ."

"GR 44," Woodward shouted. "Respond! That is an order!"

Suddenly Luc broke off his stare, tearing his eyes from the two children. He gazed fixedly at Andrew Scott's smooth, emotionless face.

Chapter Three

It took a while for the reporters assembled in the press area to get the news that whatever had been happening in the dam was at an end. They milled around morosely waiting for the next official communiqué, praying that some enterprising newsperson from CNN or the Associated Press wouldn't flush out the facts and break the story ahead of everybody else. Even though she was officially out of a job, Veronica Roberts waited with her colleagues, out of force of habit as much as anything else, but her mind was more on her own problems than on the incident at McKinley Dam.

Huey, who had worked on enough stories with Veronica to know that he shouldn't fall in love with her—though that didn't stop him from doing just that—waited with her, giving her a shoulder to cry on, although tears were not part of Ronnie Roberts's MO. She was still burning mad at the treatment she had undergone at the hands of Charles.

She paced and smoked and fulminated. Her fellow journalists had seen Veronica's pyrotechnics before so they didn't pay much attention.

"I can't believe that jerk fired me!" She sucked on a cigarette, drawing it almost down to the filter. "Hey, I was on another story. A big one."

Huey shook his head. "That's just the problem— You're *always* on another story. It's just never the story they assigned. You know, the one they pay you for. Like this one, remember?"

"This was just a hostage thing. Anybody could have done this."

"C'mon, Ronnie. International terrorists taking over the goddam McKinley Dam? That's a big story. Besides—it's the one they wanted you to cover. If they tell you to cover a dog show—you go to the dog show. Got it?"

"I don't like dogs."

"Don't be ridiculous. Everybody likes dogs."

"*I* don't," she insisted.

"Look," said Huey soothingly. "This could be the best thing to happen to you in a long time. You're overextended. You need a break. Some time off. You should go out. A little relaxation once in a while won't kill you, you know . . ." Unspoken was the suggestion that if she should need someone to relax with, then he just might be available.

Ronnie shot him a withering glance. "Don't start this again."

But Huey persisted. "He's been dead for three

years. Get over it. You have to move on. Maybe start something new." Huey was on thin ice here—Ronnie didn't like to be reminded of tragic events in her recent past, and if you pushed too hard, she could come roaring back like a bear with a sore head.

But not today. She looked sad and shook her head. "Yeah . . . I suppose. But what?"

"Something will turn up," he said, doing his best to comfort her. "Trust me."

When the Army, the local police and the FBI were good and ready, they announced that the hostage situation was at an end and that the press pool—now something like a hundred and fifty people, including camera crews and other technicians—might as well pack up and go home. Instead of defusing the tension in the air, the announcement only pumped the pressure up a couple more notches. *Now* the real story began. Just who were the terrorists? How many had lived? And, most important of all: who got into that dam, into an impossibly dangerous situation and coolly took them down?

They were promised a briefing later that day, but that wasn't good enough for a journalist wolf pack starved for news. They caught sight of Perry making for his jeep, and they fell on him like piranhas. Veronica and Huey followed with the mob—they had to. It was in their blood to follow a story.

Perry almost made it to his vehicle before being

encircled and forced to stop and answer at least some of the questions that were being hurled at him. A thicket of microphones and micro-cassette recorders were thrust into his face, and the air was alive with the flash from still cameras and the floodlights from the video recorders.

"Just who were these guys, Colonel?" yelled the guy from United Press International.

"I'm not at liberty to give out any information regarding the soldiers involved in the operation," Colonel Perry snapped back.

"Soldiers?" the UPI guy followed up. "So they are regular Army, not FBI or any other branch of law enforcement?"

Perry couldn't stand to have any of the glory go to the cops. He hesitated a moment, then said, "Affirmative."

"Can you give a unit designation? A handle? A nickname? *Anything?*" pleaded the reporter from the Las Vegas *Tribune*.

Sullivan, Perry's aide, had spent some time with the Signal Corps, press section, and it was part of his present duties to deal with the press if the occasion should ever arise. He was something of an expert in handling the media, and the Colonel, who knew nothing about reporters, was quite happy to be guided by him in matters relating to newspeople. When all these questions were fired at him, Perry instinctively looked to Sullivan for guidance, and the lieutenant nodded very slightly, giving him the go-ahead.

Colonel Perry sighed. He was dead against

giving anything to the press if he could help it. "My unit is an advance on some of the Special Force divisions that have been formed in recent years to counter sudden and extremely dangerous situations—"

"Delta Force?" yelled someone.

"Similar," conceded Perry.

"But better?"

"More . . . ah, advanced."

"Name?"

Colonel Perry looked at the press aide, who nodded.

"Universal Soldiers," he said. "Abbreviated to the designation Unisols."

"Colonel Perry," shouted the AP man on the scene. "How many Unisols were killed in the rescue?"

"None."

"Injured?"

"Negative."

"Who are they, Colonel? Can you give us any names?"

Colonel Perry had had just about all he intended to take from the press corps. "This marks a successful mission for the Universal Soldiers, a successful mission accomplished, as I have stated, without casualties or injuries. But I'm sorry, the identities of the Unisols are classified. As you can imagine, these men have wives and children waiting at home for them. I will not do anything to jeopardize their lives. Thank you." He climbed into his Jeep, the press shouting after him.

The lieutenant moved to cut them off. "There will be a complete briefing later this afternoon." He jumped into the vehicle, and the Jeep pulled through the massed crowd.

The press was disappointed to see Colonel Perry go. They had gotten him to open up a little, and each person there felt that with a little more time he would have spilled additional information about this mysterious, elite force with the flashy name. The TV lights died, the flashes stopped abruptly and tape recorders were clicked off.

A press photographer rewound his film and loaded another roll into one of the Nikons around his neck. "Great," he said in disgust to no one in particular. "Twenty exposures of some hard-ass colonel talking the Pentagon line. No Pulitzer there. If we can't shoot these guys, what the hell are we doing here? We need pictures."

A mischievous smile crossed Veronica Roberts's face. Huey saw it and he didn't like it. She started marching toward her Wagoneer, looking down the road at the retreating Jeep that carried Perry and his crew.

"Please, Ronnie," Huey implored. "Don't even *think* about it."

"Come on," she said, "we've got to hurry."

"Ronnie, I don't think we should—"

"Huey, don't be such a wimp, for God's sake."

"Hey, I got a briefing to cover and a plane to catch."

"That's right, *you've* got a briefing to cover. *You've* got a plane to catch."

"No, you too. CNA brought you out here. They've got to take you back."

"The hell with that."

"Hey, Ronnie," shouted one of the technicians working with one of the networks, "where the hell you going?"

"Back to Vegas," she called over her shoulder, hoping she didn't sound as if she was lying.

"Vegas? The briefing is here."

"Hey. Haven't you heard?"

"Heard? Heard what?"

"I've been fired."

All of the Universal Soldiers, except for the injured GR 74, had been returned to the Unisol command truck. Postoperational procedure was always a series of well-defined tasks. Casualties, if any, were removed from the unit, and the rest of the men were consigned to the cooling chamber, where Garth, Woodward and the rest of the technicians set about shutting the fighters down, putting them in human mothballs to await the next call to arms.

By the time Colonel Perry made it back to the truck, the Universal Soldiers had been stripped of their gear and seated at their places, naked, in the cooling chamber. The eleven men were lined up like chess pieces, all of them sitting erect and inert in their throne-like seats while their handlers peered at them through the monitors, checking the myriad life-sign readouts as the dense ranks of numbers and impenetrable acronyms flashed across a dozen computer screens.

One of the engineers on the project was actually inside the frigid chamber with the men, dressed in a shiny, thick protective garment and helmet—he looked like a land-bound astronaut—monitoring the temperature drop from within the room. He had done his job so many times before, he scarcely noticed the row of naked men seated in front of him, their powerful bodies crisscrossed with raw scar tissue, as if they had been stitched together by a high-tech seamstress.

Perry got to the command post just in time for the last stage of the cooling process. The voice of the man in the cooling room came through a speaker over the control consoles as he read off the temperature scales.

"At thirty below," the man intoned, "lowering to final stage of sixty degrees, sub zero . . ."

But his readings were not on Garth's mind; nor were they any concern of Woodward's. The two men had something far more intriguing to deal with. They had brought a close-up of GR 44—Luc Devreux—onto one of the screens and were peering at his impassive face with great interest, as if they had never seen him before. Both men were uneasy, anxious, a little worried. GR 44 looked the same as he always did; during the operation at the dam he had performed to plan and procedure—but he was, somehow, different . . .

"What happened?" Perry asked crisply.

Garth shrugged. "Hard to say, Colonel."

"He froze up," said Woodward.

"He was doing fine. Working like a dream, then all of a sudden he froze. We can't figure out what happened."

"How do you mean, 'froze up'?" asked Perry.

"At the end of the mission he shut down. He became completely unresponsive," explained Woodward. "Took us damn near ten minutes to get him on line again." Woodward shook his head. "It's never happened before."

"Did he overheat?"

Garth almost laughed. "Overheat? Hell, he hardly broke a sweat."

Colonel Perry leaned in close to the image of Luc Devreux and grabbed a microphone. "GR 44, why didn't you respond?"

Luc reacted slightly when he heard his name, cocking his head a little, but he didn't answer immediately.

"GR 44," Colonel Perry coaxed gently. "Why didn't you respond, back there, at the dam, during the operation?" His voice became a touch more stern. "Answer me, GR 44 . . ."

It was as if Luc couldn't quite figure out the words spoken to him. "Innocent," he said quietly.

Colonel Perry snapped off the microphone so Luc couldn't hear. The commanding officer looked to Woodward. "Innocent? What the hell does that mean?"

Woodward shrugged. "Search me, Colonel."

Perry turned back to Luc Devreux. "What do you mean, 'innocent.' GR 44? Explain that to me."

In Luc's brain he heard the faint sounds of a far-off war. He spoke groggily, as if in a deep sleep. "The town has been cleared, Sarge. These people are innocent."

"Sergeant?" Perry was puzzled. There were no ranks in the Universal Soldiers, just leaders; "sergeant" should have been a term unknown to Luc Devreux's reconstructed brain. "What sergeant? Who the hell is he talking about?"

"Could be an old memory," said Woodward.

"You mean it's just a flash?"

"Probably."

Perry relaxed. Random memory flashes were not common with the Universal Soldiers unit, but they weren't unknown. "You had me worried there for a second."

"It's probably nothing," put in Garth. "He could be building up immunities to the serum, that's all."

"Well, give 'em another jolt of serum. That should clear GR 44's brain for him."

Garth swallowed hard. No matter how many times he administered the serum to the Unisols, the process always made him feel queasy.

"Yes sir, Colonel." Garth took control of the microphone. "Okay, guys, time for a little memory clearance."

Each of the Universal Soldiers reached for a small red button set in the arm of his seat. As soon as it was pressed, the top of the backrest opened and a multipronged, spiky, silver device emerged, traveling up to the back of the soldier's head, powered by a small electric motor. The apparatus looked like the metallic hand of a robot. The steel fingers of the fist clamped firmly on the head of each man, and materializing from the palm of the contraption was a long, shiny silver hypodermic needle. The shaft jabbed hard and long into the back of the skull of each inert man, slicing through the bone of the cranium.

The image was a nightmarish one, but the Universal Soldiers didn't react to the jab deep into the soft tissue of their brains. They experienced no pain whatsoever.

Garth did. He winced and grimaced and had to turn away. He had a lifelong fear of needles and seeing a dozen driven deep into the heads of unflinching men, buried in their brains, did nothing for his phobia.

Woodward smiled when he saw his assistant's discomfort. "You'll just never get used to this part, will you?"

"Nope." Garth busied himself watching the dials on his console, paying elaborate attention to the dose of memory-clearing serum each man was getting. It helped him take his mind off the hideous scene on the screens.

"Okay," said Woodward, "that's enough."

Garth pressed a button and the needles withdrew from the back of each Unisol's head, clear liquid oozing around the shafts as they pulled out. All of the men had glazed looks in their eyes, faraway, unfocused expressions on their faces.

"I'll take over," said Colonel Perry. "GR 44, can you hear me?"

Luc nodded slowly.

"You will repeat after me . . ."

Luc nodded again, completely under the sway of the commander of his unit, a voice he was powerless in that very moment to disobey.

"You were confused," intoned Colonel Perry, like a hypnotist planting a suggestion very deeply in the brain of his hapless subject.

"I was confused," repeated Luc Devreux.

"You will clear your memory."

"Memory cleared."

Colonel Perry's voice became a little more severe, like a strict parent reprimanding an errant child. "You must follow your orders at all times. Do you understand me, GR 44?"

Luc nodded. "I must follow my orders at all times. I understand."

Colonel Perry turned the control back over to Woodward and Garth. "See," he said with a satisfied smile, "he's fine."

Woodward frowned. "Colonel Perry, I think we may have a little more of a problem here than you might think. I suggest we pull all of the units in for analysis. We can't afford to have an incident—"

"Out of the question," snapped Perry. "It took too goddam long to get this project operational. I will not authorize any change of plan. Is that clear? We admit to a mistake and we'll get shut down for good."

"Well, take GR 44 out," insisted Woodward. "We'll run some tests, just to make sure."

"No," said Woodward firmly. He glanced at Luc Devreux's face, still on the monitor. "He's fine. That's all."

"Those guys have got one hell of a mobile home," said Veronica Roberts. Hunkered down in the front seat of her Wagoneer, she swept her high-powered binoculars across the airstrip, studying the Universal Soldier command truck. They were a long way from the center of operations, having not dared drive any farther than the rampart of junk and decaying planes that ringed the airstrip.

Following Colonel Perry had been easy, and getting onto the airfield had been so simple that at first Ronnie and Huey thought they had come to the wrong place. The old barbed wire fence was rusted through in a dozen places, and security patrols appeared to be nonexistent. The Universal Soldiers had been called into action so unexpectedly and in such haste that there just hadn't been time to plan for adequate protection.

Ronnie swiveled her field glasses to a point next to the Unisol truck and spotted a couple of guards, standing around, bored out of their skulls, probably wishing away the long hours of their duty time.

"They've still got guards posted," she reported. Huey brought up the snout of his handy-cam

61

video recorder and shot a few meters of tape, just to feel as if he were doing something important.

"So what?" he said from behind the eyepiece.

"That tells me that these Unisols must still be here."

"Brilliant deduction." Both of them jumped as the beeper alarm on his wristwatch sounded.

"What the hell is that?"

Huey lowered the camera and turned off the signal. "That was final boarding for our flight out."

Veronica went back to her binoculars. "Oh that . . ."

It was kind of an odd time to bring it up, Huey thought, but this was as good a time as any to discuss his feelings for his coworker—ex-coworker—besides, he hardly ever got the chance to be alone with Veronica.

"Ronnie . . ." He struggled to find the right words, swallowing nervously. ". . . we've been working together for a long time. We're friends, right?"

Veronica was studying the C-130 transport plane, only half listening. After a long pause she answered. "Right . . ."

"Well . . . I'd like to think that we're even a little more than that."

Veronica had turned her attention back to the Unisol command truck. She couldn't get over the size of the thing and the sheer power it seemed to have packed into it. The automatic machine guns were pretty terrifying.

"Uh-huh . . ." She wasn't quite sure what Huey had said, but whatever it was, it wasn't nearly as interesting as the view through her field glasses.

He plowed on, hoping he'd be able to find the right formula to express his feelings.

"I guess, what I'm trying to say, I should have said a long time ago . . . I think it's time I told you how I really feel about you. Now, I know what you're thinking, you're thinking I sound like a greeting card. I don't mean to, it's just that what we have goes way beyond sex." He paused a moment, considering the fact that they had never actually *had* sex. He added: "Although, you have to admit, a little sex never hurt . . ."

Veronica had stopped listening altogether. A plan was forming in her mind. Lying alongside the airstrip, not far from the Universal Soldier command truck, were three long lengths of drainage pipe, about four feet in diameter. Good cover, she decided.

"You see, Ronnie—" said Huey earnestly.

She lowered the field glasses abruptly. "We're not getting anything from way out here." She stowed away her binoculars, dug in her oversized purse for a thirty-five-millimeter camera and looked for a roll of low-light-sensitive film.

It took a second or two for Huey to realize just what she had in mind. Thoughts of romance vanished, replaced with those dedicated to simple survival.

"Are you nuts?" he whispered urgently.

"No." She found the film and began loading the cylinder into the camera.

"Yes you are, if you're planning on doing what I think you are. It's bad enough we're on government property, spying on a military installation—"

She snapped the camera shut and fired off a couple of exposures, advancing the lead-up feed onto the reel. "It's the story, Huey." She adjusted the lens and the shutter speed. "You told me to find something new. Well. I've found it."

"Ronnie," he pleaded, "this is a classified military operation. You won't get within ten feet of that truck. Believe me. Those guys are probably ordered to shoot to kill."

Veronica slid out of the Wagoneer and closed the door quietly. "I love it when people tell me what I can't do. If you're so worried you can just wait here." She darted away in the darkness, keeping close to the wrecked airplanes.

Huey watched her for a second, then slumped in the seat of the car, shaking his head, not quite able to believe she was doing something so stupid. "Why," he wondered aloud, "do I always fall for the crazy ones?"

Chapter Four

The guard was just a few feet beyond the end of the decaying drainage pipe when Veronica popped out of it like a gopher out of a hole. Somewhere a few hundred yards off, a generator coughed into life, and some standing lights on the tarmac lit up, encircling the Unisol truck, swamping it in a pool of white illumination.

Using the noise of the generator as cover, she darted from the pipe, running for the shelter of the low, heavy wing of the C-130 transport plane. Hidden behind one of the engines, she adjusted her camera shutter speed to allow for the increased light, and started firing off pictures of the truck, the auto advance mechanism of the camera scarcely able to keep up with her frenzied snapping. She was sure that anyone within three hundred yards could hear the machine and the thunderous pounding of her heart. Her fingers were trembling and she was breathing fast, but she managed to get some good shots of the truck, the helicopter and a couple of the guards.

She cursed silently though. So far she had a big fat zero. A truck proved nothing at all, no matter how impressive a piece of machinery it might be. She needed the money shot, something that would get the attention of her former employers and the rest of the world.

She had steeled herself for the move out of her hiding place, to get nearer to the truck, when she saw something made her pull back. The camera went into overdrive.

Two men had trundled a large crate up to the entrance of the truck. It was a heavy steel box mounted on a dolly, and the two men labored over it, hauling it toward the ramp that led into the Universal Soldier command center. A third man, in a white lab coat, followed. He seemed to be in charge.

Garth, one of the two laboring men, shooed the other, a guard, away, then snapped open the cover of the crate, reaching inside like a traveler rooting around in his suitcase. He grimaced as he did it, and when he pulled his hands out, Veronica could see why. His hands were covered with blood, which he wiped on the towel stuck in the waistband of his fatigue pants.

The blood seemed very red in the bright light, and Veronica quickly captured the gore on film.

"Disgusting," he said aloud. "I really hate it. This part really grosses me out."

Woodward smiled. "As soon as the flotation chamber is filled we'll have to put him in."

"Oh joy," mumbled Garth. They left the crate on the tarmac and climbed back into the truck.

Veronica Roberts couldn't help herself—she wanted more; she wanted a scoop. She crept cautiously from her hiding place, making for the circle of light and the crate. She held her camera in front of her, like a weapon.

As she drew nearer, the truck video monitor closest to her swiveled around like a bird and locked on her.

She took a deep breath, opened the top of the crate and peered inside. She almost gagged, fighting with herself to keep in position. It was the chewed-up body of GR 74, the Universal Soldier who had been so ruthlessly cut down by Wagner and his gunmen. He lay packed in blood-flecked ice, his uniform stripped away, the terrible wounds on his chest plain as day.

Ronnie gritted her teeth and angled her camera. "No casualties or injuries, eh?" she whispered under her breath.

She snapped the picture. Then another. At the sound of the camera, as if the tiny noise were enough to awake a light sleeper, GR 74 opened his eyes and sat upright.

"Jesus Christ!"

The microphone on the video camera picked up her shriek and sent it back to the monitor inside the command vehicle. No one had been paying attention to the screens, but the unmistakably feminine voice ringing through the truck got everyone's sudden and undivided attention.

Veronica had decided to get the hell out of there. It was one thing to be an intrepid reporter going after the big story—it was another thing to be just plain stupid.

The video camera followed her as she ran away from the crate and the truck. Perry saw her taking to her heels.

"Who the fuck is that?" he yelled. He punched a series of buttons and replayed the tape, catching the image of Veronica snapping pictures. "Son of a bitch!" He hit the microphone button and broadcast. "Get the Unisols moving. We have an intruder. I want that woman and I want that film!"

The entire area suddenly lit up and sirens sounded. The night was alive with men and vehicles. Huey sat bolt upright in the Wagoneer and saw, in the rearview mirror, Veronica running toward the Jeep as fast as she could.

"What the hell did she do this time?" He slid into the driver's seat and fired up the powerful engine. He gunned it as Veronica, out of breath, jumped into the passenger's seat. Panting, she rewound the film, broke open the camera and stowed the film in a canister.

"So what did you get?"

She held up the film, showing it to him for a split second before stowing it inside her shirt, nestling it inside her bra. "I got redemption," she shouted. "Now let's get the hell out of here."

Huey required no further encouragement. He

stomped on the gas and the big car jolted forward, but just as they hit speed a military Jeep careened across the airstrip and shrieked to a stop in front of them. Huey hit the brakes and wrenched the wheel sharply to his left, avoiding hitting the Jeep broadside and zooming beneath the low wing of an old Dakota. There was only an inch or two of clearance, but they made it under and Huey gave the engine all the gas he had. He put a hundred yards between him and the old plane before he ran into real trouble.

A Jeep was closing on his left, forcing him off the runway and into a tall pile of old, grimy oil drums. He gunned the engine, trying to blast through the rusting wall—and he almost made it, except behind it was another pile of debris, a mound of dilapidated packing crates and old iron engine parts. He hit the immovable barrier at top speed, the force of impact jarring the Wagoneer, throwing it high into the air, the engine racing. The heavy rig flipped over, landed roof-down on the asphalt and slid for twenty yards before coming to halt.

Huey's head had smacked into the steering wheel, opening a cut at the base of his scalp. Blood oozed down his forehead into his eyes and mouth.

Veronica was not hurt but was crunched upside down in her seat. She may have been uninjured, but she was badly shaken up.

Luc, Scott and another Unisol, designated GR 55, walked up to the stricken Wagoneer, their

Heckler and Koch submachine guns at the ready. GR 55 covered the scene while Scott and Luc positioned themselves on either side of the vehicle. Then, like the jaws of life, they tore the heavy doors off their hinges, tossing the metal panels aside like pieces of litter.

Scott yanked Huey out of his seat and dumped him on the ground. Luc stood staring at Veronica, unable to move.

She managed to squirm her hand into her inner pocket and drew out a press pass and flashed it at him. She was pretty sure that it wouldn't do much good, but there was no harm in trying. Upside down in her seat, she showed the little laminated card. "Veronica Roberts," she said, "CNA."

Luc continued to stare at this curious woman, scrunched upside down in the front seat of a smashed Jeep Wagoneer.

"Well," she said, sounding a lot more courageous than she felt, "do you want to help me out of here or what?"

This roused Luc to action. He reached into the car with curious gentleness, and helped Veronica. She tumbled out of the car, stood up quickly and dusted herself off. All three of the soldiers were silent, but the weapons trained on the two intruders spoke volumes.

Veronica did her best to swing into her innocent act. "So, uh, is there a problem, gentlemen?"

At the sound of her voice all three Universal Soldiers raised their weapons and thrust them toward her. Fear flashed across Veronica's features, and pure terror pulsed through her. She had been in tight corners before, but nothing like this, and she knew she was not going to be able to talk or fake her way to freedom. She realized with a jolt that she would be lucky to get out of this one alive.

The horror and fright on her face struck Luc like a punch to the jaw. Suddenly, in his brain he saw it again—the burst of a thought from his dead past: the Vietnamese girl, frightened beyond belief, waiting for death.

Instinctively, Luc lowered his gun.

Garth's voice crackled into their headsets. "Team report."

Andrew Scott responded. "Intruders captured," he said tonelessly. "Awaiting instructions."

In the Universal Soldier command station Garth, Woodward and Colonel Perry watched the action on three different monitors.

"They got 'em," said Garth with satisfaction.

Perry's voice came over the communication gear. "Find that film," he ordered, "and bring the trespassers back to base. The woman has the film. Search her first."

Scott received his instructions and stepped toward Veronica. Before he could lay a hand on her, however, Huey scrambled to his feet and put himself between her and the massive soldier, trying in vain to protect her.

"Leave her alone," he stammered. He was still very woozy from his injuries. "She didn't do anything."

Scott stopped and stood stock-still for a moment, staring at Huey. Then, or so it seemed to Veronica, everything that happened next seemed to happen in slow motion.

Without a word, Scott pumped a single shot into Huey's head, the force of impact picking him up and throwing him against the smashed Wagoneer. He was dead before he hit the ground.

Veronica heard herself screaming, but it seemed to come from far away. The same scream roused something in Luc. As Scott aimed his weapon at Veronica, Luc saw himself raising the butt of his weapon and smashing it into Scott's cheekbone, knocking him down. It was as if he were in the past and present at the same time, watching history and re-enacting it at the same time.

As Andrew Scott toppled, Luc Devreux grabbed Veronica by the arm and ran.

It took a second for what had happened on the airstrip to register in the brains of the men watching the spectacle on the monitors in the Unisol command post. Scott's screen was a blizzard of static and interference.

Woodward reacted first. He dove for one of the microphones and yelled. "GR 13, cease fire! Cease fire!"

"What the fuck is he doing?" demanded Perry.

Garth was frantic at his console. "Squad halt! Hold your fire. Repeat! Hold your fire!"

Colonel Perry was apoplectic. "What the hell is going on out there!"

"Picture!" shouted Woodward. "Give me picture!"

Garth fell on the controls. "GR 55! Visual!"

As obedient as a piece of machinery, Universal Soldier GR 55 turned his head to catch Luc and Veronica running fast for an unattended jeep parked a few yards away. Then the automaton looked down and showed Scott on the ground, starting to get up, stumbling to his feet.

Colonel Perry started issuing orders frantically. "Stop them! Get that girl!"

"He fucking killed him," screeched Garth in amazement. "He just shot 'im."

Perry was broadcasting to all the Unisols, his hands gripped around the neck of the microphone as if trying to strangle the life out of it. "Stop the girl. Shoot if you have to!"

"Colonel!" yelled Woodward, horrified. "They'll kill her!"

Perry ignored him. "Just stop them!" he yelled into the microphone.

GR 55 followed his orders. He spun around and pumped a shot at Luc, the slug slamming into Devreux's shoulder. But the bullet passed through, never even slowing him down. He slung Veronica into the passenger seat of the Jeep like a sack of laundry, then fell behind the steering wheel, gunning the engine and zooming away, burning rubber, the engine racing.

Through GR 55's eyepiece Colonel Perry could see what was happening. "Stop him, damn it!"

Garth was helpless at his control panel. "I can't. He's simply not responding."

"He'll respond to me," growled Perry. He seized the microphone again.

The jeep was five hundred yards away from the wrecked Wagoneer when Perry's voice reached Luc Devreux. "GR 44. Stop the car. That is an order!"

At the sound of the word "order" GR 44 stood on the brake, the Jeep slithering to a halt.

"What the hell are you doing?" yelled Veronica.

"Good," said Perry's voice. "Very good. GR 44, turn the car around. You're simply confused."

Luc turned to Veronica. "I am confused," he said, as if that would explain everything.

"What? Let's go. Hit it!"

"Don't listen to her," urged Perry.

"Listen to me," she yelled. "Don't listen to *him*." She snatched the communications unit off Luc's head and tossed it over the side. "Now go!"

There was static and feedback, and when the signal had cleared, all Perry could see was a stretch of tarmac and the right front tire of the jeep, still stopped on the airstrip. "The god-damned bitch cut us off!" the colonel yelled in frustration. "I want her dead."

"I must follow orders," said Luc.

"Bullshit!" yelled Veronica. "You want an order? How about this?" She stamped on Luc's foot, flooring the gas. The Jeep peeled out with a loud

74

squeal, shooting down the tarmac, chewing up the asphalt, heading for the highway.

GR 13, aka Andrew Scott, was on his feet now, standing next to the other Unisol on the scene, GR 55. Without emotion, GR 55 watched Luc, his renegade comrade, zoom away. Scott watched too, but not without feeling; there was something in his eyes, a sign of life.

Under his breath, he whispered, "Traitor."

Colonel Perry stormed away from the command center, tossing orders over his shoulder as he went. "Pack it up," he rapped out sternly, "we're going after them."

Woodward and Garth sat still at their consoles, not moving a muscle. Perry turned back to them. "You heard me. Move it!"

Woodward spoke. "Colonel Perry, we just killed an innocent man."

Perry didn't need this, not now. He stormed back into the command center. "And just what the hell do you suggest we do, Woodward? We're supposed to sit here and let that reporter go off with one of our Unisols?"

"I warned you about this," said Woodward. He was upset and agitated, sick to his stomach at what had happened. "If you had listened to me this accident could have been avoided. It never had to turn out this way."

"Yeah," Perry shot back, "it turned out this way. It happened, okay? And now we've got to cover our asses. It's as simple as that."

"We can't just cover this up!" Woodward yelled. "We have a moral obligation to tell the truth about this. We have to face facts here."

Something about the words "moral obligation" pushed Colonel Perry to an even greater degree of cold, cruel reason. His eyes narrowed and he looked at Woodward with a lethal hatred. "You know, I thought you were more clever than that. This whole goddam program is off the shelf."

"Colonel Perry—"

Perry cut him off. "Do you really think the wimps in the Pentagon would allow the regeneration of dead soldiers?"

Suddenly, for the first time, the technicians began to realize just what they had gotten themselves into. "Do you mean to tell me," said Woodward slowly, "that you don't have full authorization for this project?"

"Oh God," whispered Garth.

"Stafford Industries wants these guys turned into American heroes and that's just what we're going to do. This whole charade is a goddamned promotional tour designed to make the Unisol program untouchable."

"Charade. . . ? Then who were the people in the dam?" asked Garth. "The terrorists?"

"Some thugs from Vegas," snapped Colonel Perry. "Told them it was part of an exercise. Paid 'em too. Told them they wouldn't get hurt."

"But they're *dead*."

"So what? Who'll miss 'em?"

"Jesus Christ," said Garth.

Woodward stood up and straightened his shoulders. "Colonel Perry, I don't think I can be part of this anymore."

"Well, Woodward, you *are* part of this. Understand me, my friend, if we are uncovered now, we're all going to jail. Got it? Understood? Just let that sink in before you make any rash decisions. Now, I'm going to get this goddam operation in fucking gear." He turned on his heel and marched out of the command center.

Garth turned to Woodward, badly shaken by all that had happened in the last few minutes. "Hold on. Jail? What the hell is he talking about? Jail?"

"Promotional tour," said Woodward sourly. "He thinks he can do for the Universal Soldiers what Saddam Hussein did for the Patriot missiles."

Chapter Five

The Jeep stormed down the empty desert high-way, zooming through the night, away from the Universal Soldier landing strip, doing seventy-five miles an hour on the flat, dead-straight road. As far as Veronica Roberts was concerned, they couldn't get away fast enough. The weight of what had just happened to her, to Huey, was beginning to sink in, and her usually steel-hard nerves were beginning to crack. She kept looking over shoulder, expecting to see the headlights of a dozen chase vehicles stabbing into the night in hot pursuit. There was nothing.

But she couldn't relax. Veronica knew that whoever those guys back there were, they weren't going to let this thing just go away. A man was dead and the man next to her was AWOL from some kind of top secret operation. *Something* was going to happen and it wasn't going to be pretty.

She had to get hold of herself, to think her way

through, to figure out some way to get safe and get safe in a hurry. She had to locate some little bit of civilization—a truck stop, a motel, a gas station—and get to a phone.

Her eyes swept the road ahead, while she prayed she would see some welcoming lights, but nothing broke the velvet darkness of the desert night.

She dug in her blazer pocket and pulled out a crumpled pack of cigarettes; then she patted her pockets, looking for matches. But there were back in her stricken Wagoneer.

"Shit," she said edgily and was about to toss the cigarettes into the rushing wind when Luc stopped her.

"There's a lighter in the dashboard," he said.

"Oh, I wouldn't have thought a Jeep had . . ." Veronica pushed the knob and with shaky hands put a cigarette to her lips. Luc observed her as if watching a rare and very curious animal from a distant continent. His gaze further unnerved her—just what she needed.

"What? What are *you* looking at?" she snapped.

He looked away.

The lighter popped and she grabbed at it, and between the jolting ride of the Jeep and her jittery hands, she had a certain amount of difficulty guiding the glowing tip to her cigarette.

She took a long, hard drag, drawing the smoke down deeply into her lungs, hoping that the shock of the nicotine would calm her unsteady nerves. But it would take more than a cigarette. She felt the sickening wave of hopelessness break over her. Her voice quavered, betraying her fear and her anxiety. Luc was staring at her again, wondering how he could comfort her.

Veronica was losing it and she started to babble. "He didn't do anything. He was just trying to protect me. Nothing but fucking animals . . ." She stuck her cigarette into her mouth and wrapped her arms around herself, as if trying to ward off the chill of the desert night air.

"How could they just kill him like that? They're not going to get away with it. I swear . . ." But her brave words were betrayed by her shaking shoulders and tears that suddenly sprung into her eyes. She broke down, covering her dirt-streaked face with her hands.

"Are you injured?" asked Luc. His eyes were watching the road now. Abruptly, he pressed down on the brake and brought the Jeep to a complete halt.

She took her hands away from her face and looked around, shooting a nervous glance over her shoulder, seized with paranoia. She fought to contain her emotions.

"What? Why did you stop?" She studied the night around the Jeep. There was no light except for the headlights, no sound except the racket of the idling engine. "What's going on?"

They were at a crossroad, a place where the wasteland highway traversed a set of old railway tracks that looked as if they hadn't seen any train traffic in twenty-five years. "Before proceeding, I must check for any approaching train."

Veronica stared at him in disbelief. Suddenly, her nerves didn't seem to be so jangled. Instead, she got mad. "Hey, pal, I've got to get to a phone—fast. Get me to a town, a gas station, something."

"Before we proceed, you must buckle your safety belt. It is regulation."

Veronica's eyes widened. "What?" She shook her head. This night was getting more and more weird. "What are you? A driver's ed. instructor?"

"It is for your safety," he said.

"You have got to be kidding."

He continued to stare at her, and she had the feeling that they would not be moving again until she did as he said. Quickly she fastened the belt.

"There," she said. "Happy now? Satisfied?"

"Yes," he said. He put the Jeep in gear and crossed the tracks. Quickly he brought the vehicle back up to speed.

Veronica pulled her tattered notebook out of the inner pocket of her CNA blazer. Angling it toward the dashboard light, she clicked her ballpoint pen and starting writing. "Listen, we've got to report this thing, now, before these bastards get away. I need some information."

"Information?" asked Luc.

"Let's start with your name."

"GR 44," said Luc.

"Is that your first name or your last?" Veronica

asked sarcastically. "And by the way? How do you spell that?"

"I am GR 44. Universal Soldier strike force."

"Don't give me this rank and serial number shit," Veronica shouted. "What's your real name?"

"GR 44," said Luc impassively.

Veronica Roberts twisted in her seat. "Well, listen, Mister Top Secret, you saved my butt back there and now you're going to have to go all the way. There's going to be a criminal investigation and some people are going to jail." She wondered if Nevada was a capital punishment state. She hoped it was. "You are going to have to testify against your own people, you know that, don't you?"

Luc listened to her words but remained dispassionate. He did not answer.

"Why'd you do it?" She drew the last of the smoke from her cigarette and then threw it out into the night. "Why did you help me out back there?"

Luc had to think hard, his mind groping for an answer. The explanation didn't come easily. He knew there was a reason for his actions, but the reply was hard to put into words. The utterance that came, though, was automatic. "My tour is up," he said automatically. "I just want to go home."

"What does that mean?" If Veronica didn't understand the answer, neither did Luc.

He struggled to understand, his brows knit in

deep concentration. "My tour's up. But . . . but I can't leave until you're safe."

She stared at him without comprehending. Suddenly she noticed that the shoulder of his uniform was sodden with blood, and gore dripped down the front of his fatigues.

"My God!" Veronica shrieked. "You've been shot!"

Luc looked down at his body, examining the blood as if it were nothing more disturbing than a soap stain. Wounds meant very little to him. This gaping hole in his shoulder caused no more discomfort than a mosquito bite.

"You must be in agony. We have got to stop that bleeding," said Veronica urgently. "Is there a first aid kit in this thing?" She turned and started rummaging in the rear seat of the Jeep. "Shit," she said, "nothing."

Luc took his own steps to attend to his wound. He punched the cigarette lighter into the dashboard. Keeping one hand on the wheel, he ripped the fabric of his uniform away from the injury. Veronica winced when she saw the gaping, bloody hole.

The lighter popped back out and Luc grabbed it. Without pausing, he jammed the hot point into the wound, and the scalding metal seared his flesh. There was a crackle as some of the shreds of skin burned away, and there was a whiff of the smell of meat broiling. Luc registered no pain at all.

Veronica screwed up her face in disgust and

looked away. "Oh my God!" She couldn't tell which she found more astounding—the disgusting thing he had done to himself or the fact that he indicated no pain at all.

Luc pulled a small spray container out of one of the pockets in his fatigues and misted the wound.

"The bleeding has stopped," he said impassively. Veronica could not tear her eyes away from his face. She was deeply frightened and had no idea what she was dealing with. Luc Devreux pressed down hard on the accelerator, and the jeep streaked through the night.

They traveled a mile or two in silence, Veronica staring at him suspiciously. Finally, unable to contain herself, she spoke.

"Your wound. Does it hurt?"

"No," said Luc.

"*Did* it hurt?"

"No."

In that moment, the engine of the Jeep coughed and the vehicle started to jolt, grinding to a halt. "What the hell is going on?" she yelled.

Luc did not look concerned. Nothing, it seemed to her, could shake him from his stolid, placid state. "We are out of gas," he said. He took the Jeep out of gear and got out, to walk to the rear of the Jeep.

"What the hell are you doing?"

Luc didn't answer. He bent over, putting his strong hands on the tail end of the Jeep. He dug his boots into the asphalt and started to push. The car rocked forward. Veronica didn't think that she could panic much more, but she managed to push her anxiety up a notch, to record levels.

Slowly, at first, then picking up speed, Luc launched the Jeep down the roadway, propelling, thrusting the heavy vehicle along. As he started to run, the Jeep seemed to be no more weighty than a wheelbarrow.

As the machine raced along the highway, Veronica managed to get hold of herself, unbuckled the seat belt and slid in behind the steering wheel, grabbing hold of it and guiding the Jeep. As the speed increased, so did her fear. She managed to take her eyes off the road to gape at the speedometer. It was rising from twenty miles an hour to twenty-five; then it hit twenty-five and kept going. As Luc hit his stride, the needle stopped and held at thirty.

Veronica held the wheel, white-knuckled. She shouted into the wind: "What have you gotten yourself into *this* time, Ronnie!"

They had hustled the Unisol squad back into the cooling chamber, as freezing coolant blasted into it. Colonel Perry and his reluctant technicians stared at Andrew Scott's image on the monitor.

"First GR 44 and now GR 13," grumbled Perry. "What the hell is going on here?"

"I don't know, Colonel. We *have* to take GR 13 out of the loop. He's unstable. A loose cannon. There's no telling what he might do the next time he's in action. We can't risk another incident.

What if he had shot one of the hostages in the dam? He *killed* a man tonight, for God's sake."

Perry turned on Woodward, fury showing plainly in his face. "Don't tell me what to do." He smacked one hand into the other. "I'm in command here. Right now I need every soldier I've got. Just double the goddam serum. All of 'em. Got it?"

"Colonel," protested Woodward, "doubling the serum would be very, very—"

"Just do it," Colonel Perry barked.

Woodward's shoulders slumped, and he turned back to the control console, beaten down by the force of Perry's anger. "Garth," he said, "you take over."

"Okay," said Garth, taking command, grabbing the communication link to the cooling chamber. "Once again, memory clearance."

Right on cue, the Unisols pushed the buttons in the arms of their seats, and the steel claws emerged immediately from the headrests. The needles pierced the skulls, and Garth, squeamish as always, turned away. The moment his eyes were averted, Scott's hand dropped away from his button. The injection device drilled the skulls of his fellow Unisols—but not his.

No one noticed.

Colonel Perry was deep in conversation with his aide, the press-handling Lieutenant Sullivan. "Her name is Veronica Roberts," said the lieutenant. "A real pain in the ass. She's a reporter for

CNA. She's made a big splash with a couple of stories this year. She was fired this afternoon."

"Good. Use that. Put it out. Use your contacts to smear her. You can handle that, can't you?"

"Yes, sir," said Lieutenant Sullivan.

"Now, let's get this show on the road. Garth, as soon as that procedure is complete, I want them back in action. Suited up, armed and ready to perform. Got it?"

"Yes, sir," said Garth quickly.

Perry swiveled around to Woodward, who was lurking in a far corner of the control room. "And you—" Perry jabbed a finger at Woodward. "You get with the program. That is an order."

"Yes, sir," said Woodward reluctantly.

An aide rushed up and handed Perry a piece of paper. "There was a tracking beacon on the Jeep, sir, and the unit in the cab has picked it up. They're moving due east about sixteen miles away. They were traveling fast, sir, but they've just slowed down considerably—possible mechanical failure."

"Then we've got them. Let's move it!"

The Universal Soldier truck management team had broken the vehicle down to its traveling size, and the giant engines were rumbling to life. On Perry's command, the behemoth roared out into the darkness.

Chapter Six

At long last, a light appeared far off along the darkened road, and Veronica could finally heave a sigh of relief. Luc was still behind, pushing for all he was worth. He too seemed to derive further strength from the sight of the roadside settlement, and he picked up the pace noticeably.

At first, they were too far off for Veronica to make out exactly what they were heading for. But, as the miles passed, she could see that they were approaching a small set of buildings—a gas station and what looked like a motel. She didn't care what it was as long as they had a phone, some connection to the outside world.

A hundred yards from the lights, Veronica could make out the name of the place: "The Gas and Crash Motel," said a flickering neon sign. There were one or two cars parked in front of the motel wing, and there were a couple of vehicles that seemed to be part of the garage—a bruised pickup and a greasy, grimy tow truck.

Luc pushed the Jeep into the garage forecourt and stopped. The minute he came to a standstill, Veronica jumped out of her seat, and she was about to bolt for the garage office when Luc grabbed her by the wrist and stopped her. He was dripping with sweat and as pale as a sheet of paper, but she hardly noticed—she had more important things on her mind.

"Hey!" she protested. "I told you. I have got to get to a phone immediately."

Luc was scanning the area, looking for trouble, anything that might suggest that Perry and his Unisols had gotten there first and laid a trap. If the Gas and Crash had seen better days, they were very much in the past. The gas station was just two battered pumps and a bucket of dirty water. The lights were off in the garage, suggesting that the dusty sign in the window—"Qualified Mechanic Always On Duty"—just might be playing fast and loose with the truth.

There was a light in the window of the motel office, but not a soul stirred. A neon Vacancy sign buzzed above the door. If the Unisols were there, waiting in ambush, Luc Devreux could not detect them.

"Look," said Veronica hotly, "I have got to make that goddamn call."

He let go of her wrist and she ran for the pay phone standing next to the garage, beside the big ice machine. Slowly, Luc walked toward the motel office.

There was a middle-aged man behind the registry counter, a seedy-looking guy in a dirty T-shirt that barely covered his beer belly. He had a well-chewed cigar butt in his mouth. Beyond the office, Luc could see an elderly woman sitting in a rundown parlor, part of the living quarters of the motel owner and his wife. The woman scarcely looked up from the TV program she was watching. It sounded like a game show.

The proprietor didn't seem all that surprised to see a fully armed Special Forces soldier walk through the front door of his seedy motel. You ran into all types in an establishment like the Gas and Crash.

"I need gas," said Luc.

The motel owner took the cigar out of his mouth and smiled, showing a row of brown teeth. "Ain't got none. Ran out of gas yesterday. Refueling truck should be here in the morning. Want to rent a room?" He examined Luc's clothes and all his hardware—the Heckler and Koch, the Colt .45 revolver, the belts of ammo and the rest of the high-tech weaponry that festooned his uniform. "Nice guns," he said.

Suddenly, the hunk of chronometer on Luc's wrist began to beep. A yellow light was flashing in the center of the dial. Luc turned off the beep, but continued to stare at the light. Sweat dripped from his forehead and fell on the floor like rain.

"Hey, pal," said the motel owner, "I don't think you look so good. You feeling okay?"

Luc grabbed a handful of sweat off his brow and ran his hand through his perspiration slicked hair, breathing deeply. "I need to cool down."

"All our rooms have air conditioning," he said. Then he winked broadly. "Got some with water beds too."

Veronica burst into the office, in a rage, storming over to the desk. "That pay phone is out of order. Do you have a phone I can use?" In case the motel owner missed the point, she stared at an old black rotary phone sitting right in front of her on the reception desk. There was a dialing lock on the face.

"Yep. I got a phone you can use."

"Great." She grabbed the handset of the black phone.

He took it out of her hand and replaced it on the cradle. "No, not that one. There's a phone in every room. Only fifty dollars a night. Talk all you want."

"I don't need a room, mister," she said through clenched teeth. "I need a phone. Why can't I use this one?"

"That phone is for employee use only. Sorry." The man smiled evilly.

Veronica was in no mood to bargain. If she had to rent a room to get the news of Huey's death out and to ensure that his killers were brought to justice, then it was worth the price of a seedy motel room.

"How much?"

"That'll be fifty dollars a night. Cash, that is. No checks, no credit cards. But seeing as there's two of you that's a double occupancy." The smile never left his face. "That's an extra ten dollars."

Veronica flipped out her wallet, peeled off the money and slammed it on the counter. "Give me the key."

The proprietor dangled the key in front of her, like a kid taunting a puppy with a treat. Just as she reached for it, he pulled it back. "There's the small matter of the key deposit."

"Jesus Christ! How much?"

"Twenty dollars."

Thoroughly annoyed, she slammed a twenty-dollar bill down on the reception desk and snatched the key.

"Have a nice stay," said the motel owner as she charged out of the office, Luc Devreux trailing along behind.

About six or seven miles down the road, the Unisol command truck ground to a halt.

In the cab of the giant vehicle Perry, sitting next to the driver, studied the red light blinking on the illuminated, computerized map mounted on the dash. The luminous red dot glowed, unmoving. It was the signal from the homing device, and it told Colonel Perry that Luc and Veronica Roberts were at the motel, the lights of which he could see just a short way up the highway.

Perry picked up the microphone and issued

orders. "We've found 'em. Get out there and do your stuff."

A moment later, the Universal Soldier squad clambered down out of their vehicle, Andrew Scott in the lead. He walked a few yards and then stopped under the telephone pole that carried the lines into the Gas and Crash motel and garage. There were five black cables. He fitted the silencer on the barrel of his weapon, snapping it firmly in place. Scott raised the weapon and with pinpoint accuracy shot out the conductors that held the lines, severing the wires. The cords parted and fell crackling to the warm asphalt; they fizzled and popped as they hit, dancing like electric serpents.

"Okay," said Perry, "Let's go in slow and take them down. Do it slow and do it right. Move out."

Veronica Roberts burst into the shabby motel room, snapping on the lights and diving for the television set. Luc, sallow-faced and unhealthy-looking, followed, stumbling slightly.

She didn't pay him any attention as she fiddled with the TV, hoping that the motel had cable so she could pick up her own station. "Maybe there's already something on the news about this mess."

There was no cable, so she had to make do with one of the networks. She plopped down on the bed, grabbing for the phone as she did so. The instant she sat down, however, she was rocked back up, pitching and rolling on the waves of a water bed.

"What the hell? Jesus! I thought these things went out with the lava lamp, disco and platform shoes."

The phone was dead in her hand. She clicked the plungers, trying to get something out of the receiver. "How the hell does this thing work? What do you have to do? Dial nine or something?" She fished around in her blazer pocket, found her cigarettes and lit one with a match from a book left on the indestructible, cast-iron night table, which was like a piece of patio furniture that had been brought indoors. Still ignoring Luc, she tried dialing a couple of numbers.

"I can't even get a tone out of this thing." She rattled the telephone, hoping that the owner would pick up at the switchboard. She watched the television out of the corner of her eye. The day's events at McKinley Dam completely dominated the news, starting with a description of the terrorist takeover.

"C'mon . . . ," she said, exhaling a cloud of smoke. She had her back to Luc, having virtually forgotten his existence.

Luc had hobbled over to the air conditioner and turned it up as high as the rickety machine would go. As the cold air billowed, he began stripping off his uniform, peeling his sweat-sodden clothes down to bare skin.

The news story shifted to the storming and liberating of the McKinley Dam. They went through the tale of the terrorists, the deaths of the hostages and the assault on the dam by an elite force of Army Special Forces commandos. There was a snippet of the impromptu press conference Colonel Perry had conducted at the dam site.

"Bastard," hissed Veronica when she saw his arrogant face.

Then: "And in a surprising development," the anchorwoman read, "a CNA cameraman, Huey Taylor, was shot and killed in a motel room in neighboring Eagle Rock City. Witnesses allege that CNA correspondent Veronica Roberts shot him after an apparent argument. Cocaine and other narcotics were found at the scene. The whereabouts of Ms. Roberts are not known at this time, and law enforcement authorities are conducting a search in central and southern Nevada . . . In other news . . ."

Veronica never head the other news. First she went very pale; then her face turned bright red as anger and hatred blazed through her. She threw the phone aside and charged for the door of the room.

"There is no way on earth they are going to get away with this."

Luc managed to tear himself away from the cold air streaming out of the vents and, buck naked, chased after her, following her out into the forecourt.

Determined and furious, Veronica was marching toward the motel office. "They can't do this to me! I won't let them! They have framed me and they won't get away with it."

Luc caught up with her and tried to drag her back into the room. "You must stay inside. Stay under cover."

She didn't even look at him. "There's got to be a phone that works in this godforsaken place." Her loud voice disturbed their neighbors, an Asian couple, who peered out their window, amazed to see a raging woman being steadfastly pursued by a huge, and very naked, man. Quickly, they shut their curtains and locked their door.

"This area is not secure," Luc insisted.

"I don't give a damn. Why the hell don't you mind your own goddamn business? If you and your crew weren't so goddamn trigger happy, Huey would be alive now and I wouldn't be in this jam."

"Please—" He snatched at her arm.

She turned to break free and saw his state of undress. Her jaw dropped and her eyes grew wide. She looked him up and down. "What the hell are you doing?"

The motel owner, standing in the open doorway of the office, wondered more or less the same thing. He leaned back into the building, gesturing and calling to his wife. "Verna, come here. You ain't gonna believe this one."

A moment later she joined her husband and looked covetously at the handsome naked man. "My . . . my . . ." she said with a happy smile.

Luc, completely unaware that he was behaving strangely, was still trying to convince Veronica to return to her room. He knew that the Unisols could not be far behind and that he and she had to stay out of sight if they were to escape, to survive. He was beginning to overheat badly, and if he was going to pull through, he needed her help.

"It is not safe for you out here."

"What? Where . . . Where are your clothes?"

"I need to cool down," he stammered. "I need . . . I need . . ."

His watch was beeping again, and this time, in place of the yellow light, a burning red danger signal flashed. Veronica reached over and touched his forehead. She pulled her hand back instantly as if she had touched a hot iron.

"Jesus, you've got one hell of a fever. You're burning up. You're reacting to that bullet wound. You've got to—"

Luc's strong legs grew wobbly and then buckled. He sank slowly to the concrete. "I need . . . ," he gasped. "I need ice. Quickly . . ."

"Can you walk?"

Luc nodded and staggered to his feet. She got under his shoulder and slowly walked him back to the motel room.

"Show's over," she called over her shoulder to the motel proprietor and his wife.

"Well, we certainly enjoyed it," said Verna.

Veronica managed to get Luc back into the room and into the bathtub. Then she grabbed the big ice bucket on the dresser and scurried to the ice machine next to the garage. There were two more plastic containers there, so she filled all three and raced back to the room, dumping the ice over Luc's blazing, feverish body. She didn't pause, but returned for more ice, running back and forth, a one-woman bucket brigade.

The motel proprietor watched her scurry to and fro, from the front desk window. "What the hell are they doing with all that ice? You think maybe I should call the police, Verna?"

His wife scarcely lifted her eyes from "Wheel of Fortune." "Earl, why don't you just get a life?"

After ten trips to the ice machine, Veronica managed to fill the tub. Luc, lying buried in the ice, reclined, finally able to relax.

"Thank you," he said.

"You save me, I save you," she said with a shrug. "I'm going to go call a doctor."

Luc started up, alarmed, the ice rattling. "No. Don't do that. You must not reveal our position."

Veronica sat down on the edge of the bathtub. "Oh, you mean you're trying to tell me something could get worse?"

"Yes," he said shortly.

"Suuure." She studied his chest, noticing the well-healed scars that crisscrossed his body.

"You must have been in one hell of an accident." But there was something missing. The bullet hole in his shoulder, the injury that had looked so gruesome an hour or two before, had entirely closed up, the skin mended like a neatly darned patch.

"Your wound," she gasped in disbelief. "It's completely healed."

"It was not a bad injury," he said. There was no emotion in his voice.

Veronica stood up, completely bewildered. "Okay. It's time to get the hell out of here. Look, I really gotta find that phone. Will you be all right?"

"I will be fine," he said. He lowered his head back onto a reef of ice behind his neck and closed his eyes.

"Okay," said Veronica, psyching herself up. "He has got to let me use that employee phone—even if I have to get a job in this goddamn place."

Purposefully, she marched back to the motel registration office, and the proprietor jumped to his feet as soon as she burst through the door. She grabbed the telephone off the hook, and before he could protest, she shouted at him. "Don't say a word."

The look in her eye told him that she was probably giving him pretty sound advice.

"What are you people doing with all that ice?" He figured that he was within his rights to ask that question at least.

"We're keeping cool with it."

"Oh," he said. "Makes sense."

Suddenly, she slammed the phone down. "This one is dead too."

"Lines must be down," said the motel keeper. "Happens a lot out here."

"No storm, though," she said, suspicious. "Nothing that would interfere with service."

"Like I said, happens all the time. Don't need a storm to bring the lines down."

"Yeah," said Veronica dubiously. "Maybe." She crossed to the window and peered out into the night. There was no one in front of the motel, and a car hadn't rattled down the country highway since they arrived. The Gas and Crash Motel was truly in the middle of nowhere.

About a hundred yards down the road, outside of the lagoon of light provided by the motel and service station, the Unisol truck lay pulled over to the side of the road, parked in the deep shadows.

The forward video monitor mounted on the cab of the truck picked up Veronica's image at the window and fastened crosshairs on the center of her forehead. The image was relayed to the eyepieces of the Universal Soldiers who had crept up to the Gas and Crash and were fanned out throughout the complex.

Colonel Perry leaned over Woodward, staring at Veronica's face on the monitor. "Not yet," he instructed. "Don't take her out yet. Don't let him know we're coming. Wait until she goes back to the room. Wait until they're together. Then we'll take them both out."

Woodward nodded. He spoke into the microphone. "Hold fire. Repeat: hold fire."

The huge, fast brain of the computer worked with the video equipment, and in a second or two a complete, detailed schematic of the entire motel flashed up on a second monitor, Garth's station. The sophisticated seeing equipment in the Unisol van then swept over the structure, bombarding the edifice with microwaves, sensing the location of every person in the building, a lighted spot marking the position of every individual. It locked on Veronica's room and a red dot blinked on and off, showing the exact whereabouts of Luc, sunk in his bathtub full of ice.

Garth smiled to himself. Maybe he didn't like Perry or his crazy scheme, but he was something of a connoisseur of high-tech equipment and the truck was performing exactly to specification.

"We've picked up GR 44." He took up his own microphone. "GR 44 is located first room, northwestern corner." He clicked off the transmitter and turned to Woodward. "He's taking a bath. Cooling down. Vulnerable. Piece of cake."

Woodward shook his head. "Don't be so sure. Remember, he's a Unisol."

Garth refused to be convinced. He was absolutely sure that Luc's minutes were numbered. All of his erstwhile colleagues were in position, ready and waiting for the order to attack. When it came, he was sure the Unisols would execute their orders to the letter. "He's a sitting duck," Garth said confidently. "Trust me on that."

Chapter Seven

Veronica made her way back to the room she shared with Luc Devreux, the nagging suspicion that *something* odd was happening ricocheting in her brain. She knew little—nothing really—about the Unisols, but she knew that her companion was worried about them and she had seen them in ruthless action. They *had* to be coming after them; they must be out there somewhere—but, for the last few hours, they had been left alone, unmolested. She locked the door.

The television still blared, but the news had ended and a documentary had come on, a program about the Vietnam War. There was old footage of President Richard Nixon, grainy color film of the President announcing his decision to mine Haiphong Harbor in North Vietnam in May of 1972.

Luc had gotten out of the bathtub full of ice, toweled himself dry and dressed again. He sat on the edge of the bed, his submachine gun close at hand, watching the screen intently. He recognized the former president, but when the show switched to an interview with Nixon in the present day, as he defended the conduct of the war twenty years before, Luc shuddered. The President looked so much older! Luc's eyes grew wide, and his gaze was transfixed by the lined, jowly face of Richard Nixon.

He stood and stared at himself in the mirror, touching his face, amazed at his own appearance. His young, smooth face stared back at him. How was it possible that he had not aged a day and Nixon was an old man?

"Checking for gray hairs?" asked Veronica with a lightheartedness she didn't feel. She glanced out the window. "Something is wrong," she said soberly.

But Luc was not listening. He had turned back to the TV and was watching, engrossed by the footage on the screen. The documentary was coming to an end, and it was showing the tragic denouement of the war in Vietnam. The American withdrawal—file film of happy American GIs lining up to board olive-drab Boeing 707s, the soldiers flashing the peace sign at the camera—was followed by the nightmare images of the helicopters landing on the US Embassy roof in Saigon, airlifting out the last Americans while the frenzied, hysterical Vietnamese tried to cling to the skids.

The film cut to the Vietnam War Memorial in Washington, D.C., the silent, black marble vee, half-submerged in the cool green grass of the nation's capital. The announcer explained that the names of the fifty-eight thousand American dead were inscribed on the long, somber stone.

"Are you okay?" asked Veronica. As if either of us are, she thought.

The documentary had finished and the credits were rolling, the sound track blaring Jimi Hendrix's wild, sixties rendition of "The Star Spangled Banner." The words of the narrator were ringing in his ears, drowning out Hendrix's savage guitar.

"The war is over," Luc said slowly.

Veronica didn't make the connection between the TV show and Luc's past. "Maybe not. Something strange is going on. Every phone in the place is dead."

These few words brought Luc back to the present and the deadly predicament he and Veronica were in. He stood and went to the door, standing next to Veronica, bending down slightly and listening intently. Suddenly, he wrapped his arms around Veronica and pulled her roughly to the shag-carpeted floor, rolling on top of her.

Veronica looked at him as if he had suddenly lost his mind. "Just what the hell do you think you're doing?"

The answer to her question came from outside the room. No sooner had she uttered the words, than the entire room exploded in a hail of gunfire. Bullets slammed through the weak Sheetrock walls and blew out the windows, shredding the dusty drapes. Round after round punched into the room, perforating everything in their paths. A line of bullets stitched across the water bed, and water gushed up as if from a geyser. The mirror, the dresser and an old armchair were shredded in the hot hail and collapsed to the floor, a heap of rubble.

Luc saw that bullets were puncturing the room from both sides, so there was no getting out of there through the bathroom window. He could imagine what was going on—the Unisols had divided into two teams and were raking the room from both sides, hoping to catch them in a deadly cross fire.

There was only one way out. He grabbed the cast-iron end table by the leg and swung it hard against the wall, smashing a ragged hole in the rickety plasterboard, shattering the barrier between his room and the motel bedroom next door.

He threw his weight against the jagged opening, crashing through to the next room. His neighbors, the Asian couple who had seen Luc naked a few minutes before, were under the covers of their bed. Until a few moments before, when the machine-gun barrage opened up, they had been making love. Now, naked under the sheets, they peered apprehensively at Luc as he burst through the walls. The woman whimpered and the man shouted something in Japanese.

"Come on," Luc yelled to Veronica. She was still cowering in the room.

From beneath the storm of gunfire, Veronica

gathered her nerves and dove for the hole, tumbling into the bedroom. Just as she hit the ground, there was a momentary pause in the firing. Then it started again—gunfire raking both sides of the Japanese couple's room. The hapless man and his mate screamed in terror and dove for cover.

Luc threw himself against the next wall, fracturing it with a vicious body check and crashing through to the other side. Then he pulled Veronica after him.

The next room was empty of guests, but a moment after Luc crashed into it, it was alive with gunfire. He ran at the next wall and slammed into it, but this time, instead of crashing through, he bounced off it. This was the last wall of the motel, a load-bearing wall. Luc stared at it a moment, puzzled.

"Go on," said Veronica, "knock it down."

The room was being shredded by wild gunfire, and a Unisol was kicking in the door of their original room, searching the premises for signs of life—or death.

In the truck, Garth scanned the hotel building and picked up on the stone wall. "Last wall identified. Solid concrete. He ain't going nowhere." He turned to Woodward with an "I told you so" look on his face. "We got 'em trapped."

As Scott and two more Unisols tramped through the rooms, the only bodies they could find were the two Japanese tourists, still cowering beneath covers. The three men spread through the wrecked rooms, spraying each with gunfire—under the beds, into the ceiling, lacerating the closets. But Luc and Veronica had vanished. Stymied, the Unisols stood in each smoking room, not quite sure what to do next.

Scott snapped on his communication set. "We've lost them."

"That's impossible!" shouted Colonel Perry. "Garth! Tracking."

Garth dove for the controls, recalibrating, punching up the images of the motel, scanning every room. The only glowing spots on the readout were two heat points marking the whereabouts of the Japanese tourists—they were huddled so close that the two dots had melded together.

The Unisols had stopped firing now and were tramping back and forth through the wrecked rooms, turning over furniture and ransacking the bathrooms. The Japanese tourists gawked at the big men—scared of them, of course, but just as scared of the two people—Luc and Veronica—hiding under the covers of their bed. Luc had his pistol jammed into the man's side.

The moment the Unisols left the room, Luc whispered to the trembling tourists. "Do you have a car?"

The man was unable to speak. He just nodded vigorously and snatched the keys off the night table next to the bed.

Luc and Veronica tumbled out of the bed and lay flat on the floor, listening for a second. Then they started crawling toward the door. Veronica looked back over her shoulder at the two terrified tourists.

"I'm sorry," she said in an embarrassed whisper. "I'm so sorry."

"No time for that," said Luc, grabbing her by the wrist and pulling her from the room.

They ran across the motel parking lot and jumped in the white Chevy parked there.

Garth caught them on the monitor. He grabbed for the microphone. "They're leaving the motel! They've got a car. White Chevrolet."

Scott got the word and bolted from the room, his weapon at the ready, the other Unisols quickly following.

The Chevrolet streaked across the plaza, the engine roaring, Luc downshifting quickly, jamming the accelerator pedal all the way to the floor. The car peeled out, leaving a long strip of smoking black rubber on the cracked concrete.

Scott came tearing out of the motel, the weapon in his arms chattering, flinging a stream of bullets after the retreating automobile. The slugs crashed into the back window, smashing the safety glass into a million diamond fragments. Bullets whipped through the car, burying themselves in the dashboard and the upholstery. Veronica hit the floor, falling down beneath the dashboard.

The car fishtailed wildly as it zoomed along, aimed now at the office of the motel. The owner stood in the window, eyes wide, captivated by the phenomenon unfolding in front of his broken-down motel. As the Chevy skyrocketed toward him, Luc leaned on the horn, jolting the man from his horror-induced trance. It dawned on the man that the Chevy was headed his way—and that it had no intention of stopping.

At the last possible moment, he dove to one side, getting out of the way of the onrushing car just in time. The Chevy crashed through the window, barreled across the office—desks, chairs, papers and potted plants flying. Luc, his arms locked on the wheel, just kept on going, smashing through the wall into the living room of the owner's house and blowing by his wife, still sitting at the television set.

"Mercy!" she screamed as the car blew by.

The car shattered the back wall of the house and burst out into the fresh air, veered right and bumped back onto the highway, roaring into the darkness.

Scott and his Unisols crashes into the demolished rooms, their weapons spraying the retreating car with automatic fire.

Woodward's frantic voice came over the headphones. "Hold your fire! Hold your fire! Cease firing! There are innocent bystanders in your line of fire."

Like attack dogs called off by their trainer, all of the Unisols stopped firing and started trotting obediently toward the truck. All of the soldiers—except Scott. He stared after the escaping automobile with hate in his eyes. He was just as efficient a soldier as the others—but now he was different. The other Unisols were programmed to kill; Scott was beginning to kill because he liked it. Unlike his peers, Scott was beginning to take things personally. He was beginning to feel something denied to the Unisols for twenty years—hate, envy, rivalry. He was beginning to feel emotion.

The instant the firing stopped, Colonel Perry, Woodward and Garth got out of the command truck to inspect the smoking ruin of the Gas and Crash Motel.

They started with the motel room, the one which until recently had been occupied by Luc Devreux and Veronica Roberts. The bedroom was an awful shattered mess. There was glass and chewed-up plaster everywhere, and a few inches of dirty water soaked the red shag carpet.

Perry was the first into the bathroom, staring at the fast-melting ice still in the bullet-nicked bathtub.

"Woodward," he shouted, "get in here."

Woodward walked into the bathroom and took in the scene in a glance. He looked impressed. "Ice. He's trying to cool himself down. He's thinking on his feet. Improvising. Catching him isn't going to be quite so easy as you thought."

Perry was furious. "Goddammit!" he said. Then he turned on his heel and strode out of the room.

The Unisols had corralled the four people in the hotel—the owner and his wife and the two unfortunate Japanese tourists. The soldiers had them under loose guard, standing in front of the demolished office.

Scott was in command, but he wasn't paying any attention to the captives. He was still staring down the road, silently radiating hate.

As Perry walked by him, he rapped out an order. "GR 13. Execute erasure order. Priority ten."

Scott didn't react as he should have. Normally, a Unisol jumped at the sound of Perry's voice, but Scott didn't respond at all. He just continued to gaze down the road.

Perry stopped dead in his tracks, amazed. Just what the hell was going on? First GR 44 flips out and runs amok—now GR 13, his most accomplished Unisol, was not responding to a direct order. Right then Perry felt as if this night would never end.

"GR 13," he shouted harshly, "that's an order. Do you hear me?"

Reluctantly, Scott slowly tore his eyes from the dark horizon and nodded at the commander of the unit. "Order acknowledged, sir," he said quietly.

"Then get to it," said Perry sternly.

"Yes, sir."

Woodward, trailing behind Perry like a gundog, saw Scott's reluctant obedience, and he looked worriedly at GR 13, thinking the same as Perry. The program was beginning to unravel, and that spelled trouble for all of them.

The motel owner and his wife were staring at the devastation of their little business. The glass and rubble were all over the place, the whole building sagging and creaking ominously, as if it would come crashing down at any moment.

The old lady was not about to let her husband off the hook on this one. "Well, I sure hope you got the security deposit from those folks," she said sarcastically.

"Come on, Verna," said her husband. "Gimme a break for once in your life."

Scott walked up to them. "I'm here to help you folks. I'm going to assist you in the cleanup."

The motel owner's face brightened. If they were going to help out, maybe they would get around to mentioning paying damages too. This was plainly some kind of government operation, and the government had funds to pay off injured citizens and their damaged property.

"He stole my car," shouted the Japanese tourist. "Rental! Hertz!"

Scott smiled reassuringly. "We're going to take care of you too, sir."

The motel owner's smile broadened. "See, Verna, everything is going to be okay." He turned to Scott. "That's mighty considerate of you, son."

"Don't mention it," said Scott. Suddenly, he raised his Heckler and Koch and squeezed off two quick rounds, blowing the motel owner and his wife away, two clean shots to the head. They fell in a jumble of arms and legs.

The two tourists screamed, and Scott whipped around and dropped both of them as efficiently as he had the other two.

Woodward, almost back at the truck, heard the shots and instantly knew what had happened. "Colonel Perry! This has got to stop!"

"Don't bother me with details, Woodward," he growled. "I've got more important things to do."

Chapter Eight

Luc's eyes were locked on the road as he drove the Chevrolet at the limit of its powers straight into the rising sun. Veronica stole a quick glance at his impassive face, marveling at his control, not quite able to believe that he was completely unruffled by the firestorm they had escaped by an eyelash.

For her part, Veronica was jumpy, scarcely able to sit still in her seat, the adrenaline pumping through her body. She kept shooting looks over her shoulder, sure that she would see the lights of the Unisol truck bearing down on them. She was split. On the one hand, she was scared, more terrified than she had ever been before; on the other, she was excited, pumped up by the action and thrilled with the idea that she was probably on the verge of breaking the biggest story of her career—a secret government program that killed civilians and ran roughshod over anything or anybody that got in its way. Then a thought brought her down: she would break the biggest story of her career—if she lived to tell the story. The fear was cold in the pit of her stomach.

"You sure they're not following us?"

"No," said Luc quietly.

Veronica rolled her eyes. "You are such a comfort."

He didn't take his eyes off the road. "Buckle up."

"I'm fine."

"It's for your safety."

Veronica laughed sarcastically. "Oh. All I have to do is buckle my seat belt and that'll make me immune to bullets?"

"We are traveling very fast. You must buckle your seat belt."

"How can you be so goddam calm?" she spat back. "Your buddies back there just shot enough ammo at us to destroy Eastern Europe, and you're bitching about a goddam seat belt? I don't believe it!"

Luc took his eyes off the road and stared at her coldly. There was something in that look that frightened her. Quickly, she fastened the belt and flashed him a smile. "There. Okay? Are you happy now?"

Luc turned his gaze back to the road. He looked calm to Veronica, but within, he was wrestling with himself, trying to make sense out of the fragments of memories that kept flashing in his mind like disjointed lightning. He tried to cast his mind back, attempting to assemble the shards of his recollections and fit them with one another, as if putting together a mental puzzle. He had to gather his thoughts and figure out what had happened to him. The key to his past lay locked within his own mind.

Veronica found his steadfast silence slightly unnerving. She too wanted to know what was going on, and she couldn't help but feel that he had all the answers. She peppered him with questions, demanding an explanation.

"Okay, Mister Top Secret, I want some answers. You push a car faster than my mother drives, you use ice the way other people use Band-Aids, you knock down walls like Lawrence Taylor hits quarterbacks and you have amazing powers of recovery . . ." She remembered his rapt attention to the television set. "I'll give you this, you seem to love TV. But it doesn't tell me anything. Now, just who the hell are you?"

Luc did not answer. She let a full mile pass before speaking again. She was quieter this time, more measured, almost respectful.

"Okay." She took a deep breath and swallowed her anger. "I'm sorry. Don't get me wrong. I'm actually very grateful. But . . ." She shrugged her shoulders. "You keep risking yourself for me and I still don't know why."

This time she got a response, but it was an answer that didn't make much sense to either of them. "My tour is up. But I can't leave until you're safe."

"You mean you're not part of the Unisol program anymore? Why?"

Luc just shook his head, unable to answer her.

"You're not much of a talker, are you? Are you doing that name, rank and serial thing on me again or is it that you just don't know?" She stared at him a moment and then tried again. "Okay. Let's start off slow. How long were you a member of the strike force?"

Luc looked straight ahead, as if he hadn't heard a single word she said.

She was getting frustrated, but she managed to fight down her anger. "Look, this is how it works—all you have to do is tell me that something is off the record and I won't use it. I promise. Let's talk about you. Are you from France? French Canadian, maybe?"

Luc looked at her, puzzled, and touched the American flag sewn onto his uniform. "I am American," he said.

"Now, sure you are. But like they say, every American came from someplace else. I mean, I figure you must be French or something like that because of your accent."

Luc was mystified by her question. "What accent?"

Veronica bore down, pushing him with her words. "You got a family? Friends? A dog? Is there a Mrs. 44?"

Something she said made him wince and turn away. She sensed she was on to something and suddenly smelling blood, Veronica closed in. She pressed on his memory, as if putting pressure on a bruise.

"Are you avoiding my questions or don't you know?" Interrogation was her weapon and she used it as effectively as he used his submachine gun. "Where were you born? Who are your parents? Where are they? Do you even *have* a mother and father? Maybe you're an orphan. Did you ever consider that?" Her voice became harsher and tougher. The anger and emotion generated in the last few hellish hours was welling up in her, and she was powerless to cap it. "What do you know about yourself? Do you know anything at all?"

Suddenly, Luc stomped on the brakes, and the car screamed as it slid down the asphalt on locked wheels. The automobile rocked to a halt. Luc's hands were still curled tightly around the wheel, and he stared through the window, his visage impassive as if carved in granite. Then he turned to her, his face softening. Something was going on deep inside of him. He looked, for a second or two, naive, guileless, innocent, almost vulnerable, unprotected, exposed. Veronica was touched. For a moment this massive, cold warrior looked like a child who had lost his way.

"The only thing I remember is . . ." He had to force the words out of his mouth. "The only thing I know for sure is that I . . . I died."

Abruptly, he threw open the door of the car and walked a few yards on the roadway, breathing deeply, filling his lungs with the cool predawn air.

Veronica slipped out of the car and came near him, wanting to comfort him.

"My God," she said softly, "what have they done to you?"

For the first time in his new life, Luc Devreux looked scared, not for the future but for the past that had been stolen from him.

"I don't know," he said quietly, dejected.

"Did they hurt you?"

"I don't know."

"How did you . . . die?"

"I *don't* know."

He looked down the road, back the way they had come. The lights of the Unisol truck had appeared far away on the highway horizon, the bright beams bayoneting the fast-vanishing blackness of the night.

"I don't know the answers to any of it." He looked to the rays of light getting larger and larger. His expression darkened and he squared his shoulders, his vulnerability suddenly gone. "But I'm going to find out."

The sun was above the horizon by the time Luc Devreux and Veronica Roberts reached the next service station, a mile or two farther along the highway. The place wasn't in much better shape than the late Gas and Crash: a couple of gas pumps, an air hose, a ramshackle office, a decrepit service area and a pair of service bays, one with a hydraulic lift. The place looked as if it had been frozen in time. In front of the office was one of those old, bulky, battered blue and white Pepsi coolers with a sliding top. It was half-filled with cold water and ice and a few long-neck bottles of Pepsi poking through the water. Next to it stood a weather-beaten, rusting tin cutout of a jaunty-looking service station attendant, circa 1950, with a black bow tie and a perky smile. Written on his metal chest in flowing tin script were the words "It's our pleasure to serve you!" And then, under that, was "Esso! Service with a smile!"

The actual attendant wasn't so lighthearted or so spic and span. It was very early in the morning, and the sound of the car pulling into the station had roused him from sleep. He was not used to customers so early in the morning, and he did not look ready for business at the crack of dawn. He shuffled out of the office, scratching the stubble on his chin, and before serving them, he paused to turn out the kerosene lamp, with a red chimney, that sat on the Pepsi cooler.

He seemed to have some kind of phobia about fire, because the first thing he said to his first customers of the day was "Hey, lady, no smoking by the gas pumps."

Veronica rolled her eyes, but rather than waste a perfectly good, just lit cigarette, she slipped out of the car and walked fifteen or twenty yards away from the gasoline pumps. She parked herself in the sun and puffed away.

Luc sat behind the wheel for a moment, thinking and absentmindedly watching the gas station attendant pump gas into the dusty car. Suddenly, he jumped out of the car, stalked over to Veronica and seized her, taking her hand and pulling her toward the men's room of the gas station. He took the cigarette out of her mouth and tossed it away.

Up to that moment, Veronica had been convinced that there was nothing more Luc Devreux could do that would surprise or startle her.

"Jesus Christ!" she yelped. "What the hell are you doing?" She tried to dig her heels into the dust, but he dragged her purposefully toward the gas station bathroom.

"I need you." He shouldered open the restroom door and pulled her into the grimy enclosure.

Veronica was flustered, panicky, completely misunderstanding his intentions. "Whoa, no way. Let go of me."

"I need you to *help* me." He pushed her into the corner, leaned back against the door and started fumbling with the straps and zippers of his uniform.

"Sorry," she said firmly, "I can't help you with *that*." She watched him stripping off his clothing. "Not this again," she groaned.

"There must be a tracking device planted on me somewhere."

"A tracking device? A tracking device and you don't know where it is? Maybe it's in one of those pockets."

"No, it's not in the uniform. It's *in* me. It's hidden in my body somewhere. You must find it."

"Oh, please . . ."

He was totally nude now, completely unselfconscious about his nakedness. He placed her hands on his bare chest. "You must find it because as long as it is in me they will be able to track us down."

"Find it? How can I find it?"

He took her fingertips and pressed them into his flesh. "Dig like this. It must be close to the surface."

"But what is it?"

"It must be some kind of transmitter. Look for something unusual. Something that's not supposed to be there. Something out of the ordinary. Something hard."

Veronica was seeing his childlike side again. It struck her that his lack of self-consciousness was entirely naive, unaware that there was any breach of conventional propriety in appearing undressed. Veronica realized that Luc had absolutely no idea what should or shouldn't be on his body.

She tried not to look at him, as her hands ran down the front of his body. The plates of his chest were hard, but human. Suddenly, her hands closed around something that was large and male. Her eyes widened.

"Wow, the size of this thing—"

Luc looked puzzled. "That is not supposed to be there?"

Veronica could not help staring at the organ in her grasp, feeling a couple of years of hormone buildup flustering her. Her cheeks were burning bright red. "Ah, no," she stammered. "This is just, uh, fine. Nothing wrong with that. Far from it."

"Then continue," Luc ordered.

"Right," said Veronica. She switched to his back and worked her way down his spine, over his buttocks, then stopped at a point on the rear side of his leg, midway between his ass and his knee. She probed, exploring one spot with her fingertips. "I think," she said a little uncertainly, "I think I found something here, on the back of your thigh."

Luc did not hesitate. He slipped his finely honed bayonet out of its sheath and handed it to her. "Cut it out."

She shook her head. "What? I can't . . . I . . ."

"You *must* do it."

"No way," she said flatly. "*You* do it."

"I can't reach. You have to get that thing out of me; otherwise they will find us. And when they find us, they'll kill us." He was not being melodramatic. It was a simple statement of fact.

When it was put that way, Veronica saw that she had no choice but to do as he said. She took the razor-sharp knife and gingerly scratched at his skin, grazing it slightly, opening up a wound no deeper than a scrape.

"Just *do* it," he urged through gritted teeth.

"I can't," she whimpered. "I've never done anything like this before."

"Please," he said, imploring her. "You must do it quickly. Cut."

Veronica took a deep breath, steeled herself and jabbed hard with the keen point. Luc jumped when he felt the steel split his flesh. He was surprised to feel pain—but also strangely reassured by it. The pain brought back the fluttering shadows of long-buried memories.

Veronica jumped when he winced. "Sorry. I didn't mean to hurt you." Then it dawned on her that he hadn't flinched from a deep bullet wound to the shoulder, but now a jab in the back of the leg was causing him pain. "You felt that?"

"It doesn't matter. Find it, hurry."

She had opened an incision in his leg and was trying to scoop out a tiny metal object with the point of the bayonet, using it like a lancet. But the transmitter either slipped away from the tip of the knife or, when she had cornered it, wouldn't budge. "I can't get hold of it," she said desperately. "It's stuck."

"Use your fingers," he said.

Reluctantly, queasily, she thrust her fingers into his leg, poking for the device. His blood was warm on her fingers and it flowed slickly over her hand. "This is so gross," she said emphatically. "Really disgusting."

But she had a grip on the transmitter and she gave a tug, pulling the gadget. She tore at the thing and finally drew it out of his leg, a short cord hanging between the transmitter and the wound. She jerked and pulled out a spiky anchor, oily with blood. It dangled in the air. "I think I'm going to be sick."

"No time," said Luc, starting to pull on his clothes.

The Unisol truck came to a halt a few hundred yards from the gas station. No one emerged from the enormous vehicle while the sensors went over the dilapidated gas station.

Woodward and Colonel Perry were bent over the computer consoles, watching as Garth's fingers flew over the keyboard, cataloging the data and speeding it through the powerful brain of the machine for analysis. Almost instantly the raw statistics were digested then flashed back onto the screen. "They've stopped. They're in the gas station."

"Okay," said Perry. "No screwups this time. We take it slow and steady. I want to know everything about that shit hole before we move in. I want a full scan this time. Got it?"

"Roger, Colonel," said Garth crisply. "I'm enabling the infrared."

The monitors on the exterior of the truck swiveled and scrutinized the landscape, the charged and powerful eyes sweeping over the whole scene, reading and studying everything in their electronic arc. The color images on the screen ran from dark, registering extreme cold, as in the ice chest, up to bright red, showing the hot spots in the vista.

The Chevrolet showed up a pale blue, as did the structure of the garage itself.

"Bump it up," said Colonel Perry. "I want you to scan for body heat only."

Garth nodded to himself and hit a couple of buttons. "Scanning for body heat," he repeated.

The eye locked on the bathroom, and an identifying beep sounded long and high in the control chamber. An image appeared on the monitor screen, the rough outline of a man.

Garth laughed. "There he is. Got 'em."

"Arms?"

The technician focused the image as best he could, sharpening the picture, bringing in the outline of a gun. Information chattered across the screen, identifying the weapon. "Pistol," said Garth, "and it's fully loaded." He turned to Colonel Perry. "It's one of ours. It's a desert Eagle, semi-automatic. That's got to be him."

Colonel Perry nodded. "Good. There aren't going to be any screwups this time. I'm going to lead this mission myself."

He walked to the rear of the truck, leading the Unisols out into the cool morning. They stood in a circle around him, snapping on their gear, checking their weapons and tuning their communication headsets into the aligning tone put out by Garth at his controls. Like a quarterback huddling with his offensive line, Perry whispered instructions to his emotionless soldiers. All of the men stared at him with the devotion of pets—all except Scott, who craned his neck, trying to get a look at the gas station, edgy and nervous, itching to go into battle.

"There are going to be three teams," Colonel Perry muttered. "North, south and east. Converge on my command. Not before. Got it?"

The Unisols nodded and moved out. Perry took cover in the shadow of the truck and watched as his men moved in on the gas station. Two of the teams circled round and came in from either end. Scott, a team of one, made straight for the wooden door.

When he saw that his men were in position, Perry checked with Garth and Woodward.

"He still there? Has he moved?"

Woodward's voice came back at once. "Negative, Colonel."

"Good." He was about to give the order when he noticed something that made him furious. "GR 13. You're out of position! Goddammit!"

Scott had stopped by the ice chest, noticing a small pile of ice on the ground next to the heavy case. He stared at the ice, trying to make sense of it.

Perry's voice stung him. "GR 13! Get in position! That is a direct order!"

Grudgingly, Scott broke off his investigation and joined the rest of his team.

Colonel Perry swore under his breath. As soon as this operation was through, he was going to pull that GR 13 and give him a brainwashing, but *good*. He wished he could do it right now, but he needed every single member of his deadly squad.

He checked one last time before giving the order. "Still there, Woodward?"

"Affirmative," came the reply.

Good enough. "All teams. Converge."

It was like watching a whole set of life-like mechanical toys suddenly being switched on. The Unisols sprung into life, crashing through the door of the bathroom, their weapons spitting bullets.

The first soldier into the room, GR 61, strode over to a stall and kicked open the sagging door, the rotting old wood tearing away from its hinges and falling inward.

The Unisol registered a figure and fired, blasting in the throat the outline that was perched on the grimy toilet. But instead of hitting flesh and bone, his bullets smashed into the tin form of the Esso advertisement, the rusting cutout of the old-time filling station attendant that Luc had dragged in from outside. Dangling from the tin bow tie was the bloody homing device, still performing faithfully, even though it had been torn from its victim's body. Luc's pistol was tied to the hand of the dummy, and the whole thing was kept warm—and thus attracted and fooled the sensors—by one of the oil lamps that the attendant had put out when Luc and Veronica first pulled into the service station.

One of the bullets had hit the tin reservoir, and another had smashed the glass chimney of the lamp. Oil was flowing out of the tank, a steady steam pooling on the bathroom floor and out the main door of the lavatory. Then with a flash it caught, a sharp, hot line of fire that raced between the spread legs of the Unisol and out of the room.

In the Unisol command truck, the infrared sensors were going berserk, the cool blue tones on the monitors changing to a blazing red. "Fuck me!" Garth shrieked. "Colonel Perry, we got a major, major problem!"

Perry had already seen the dry timbers of the gas station going up, black smoke curling into the air. "Roger that," was his laconic reply.

The oil and kerosene reserves packed in the filling station storeroom erupted in a deluge of flame and acrid black smoke. For a second, every person on the premises froze, waiting to see what cataclysm would befall them next. The Unisol squad, trained to act, not command, to take and execute orders, not think them up, seemed paralyzed, lost without directives from their human leader.

The flammable material in the garage was exploding in waves, blasting like a series of chaotic explosions, heat and flame surging toward the gas pumps and the conduit to the giant storage tanks.

As if trying to resist the inferno, the old pumps buckled and twisted in the wave of flame; then, seeming to give up in the fight against the inexorable fire, they blew, acting as a fuse for the pools of gasoline buried in the concrete.

A fireball engulfed the building, and the three Unisols closest to the conflagration caught fire fast and burned bright, the fat beneath their skin acting like tallow.

"The coolants!" Colonel Perry screamed into his headset. "Quick!"

A second later, the technicians rushed out of the truck, trundling two high-tech fire extinguishers. The three burning Unisols dropped to the ground and tried to roll out the flames, but the fire had them in its grip. Through the crackling blaze, Perry could see the skin melting off their bones. He seized one of the coolant canisters and turned the nozzle on the nearest man, spraying the burning soldier at full force.

All was confusion. Between the voracious fire, brighter than the morning sun, the burning men and the indecision of the remaining men, no one was watching the Pepsi cooler. In the midst of all the bedlam, the lid of the cooler popped opened and Luc jumped out, pulling Veronica after him. As soon as she had emerged from the swamp of ice cubes, frigid water and bobbing Pepsi bottles, the garage owner surfaced. His eyes nearly popped out of his head when he saw his blazing business.

"Don't hang around," Veronica told him. "Just get the hell out of here."

The man looked at the burning buildings and bodies and needed no further encouragement to save his skin. He took off, running for the rocky hills behind the filling station.

Luc and Veronica had similar plans—except that before they made their escape, they fell on the Unisol command truck, storming into the unattended control room and scooping up armfuls of documents and manuals in file folders that littered the room.

Luc was the more efficient of the two, grabbing sheafs of papers and reports while Veronica stumbled around the truck, staring at its elaborate interior in awe. On the banks of monitors she could see the flaming chaos outside.

Woodward and Garth were frantically spraying coolant over two of the Unisols while Perry yanked another from the flames. Their voices were loud and clear in the speakers that were scattered around the room.

"We're gonna lose at least two of 'em," yelled Garth. "They're burned bad." The body at his feet was revolting to look at. The skin had been flayed off the bone by the flames and singed organs were oozing through the skeleton.

"At forty million bucks apiece we can't afford to lose any of 'em," screamed Colonel Perry. "Use more of that goddam coolant."

Veronica was transfixed. "Forty million bucks apiece?" she whispered in amazement.

Luc grabbed her roughly by the shoulders. "We have to get out of here."

Veronica couldn't agree more. "Right."

They all but fell out of the truck and escaped in a pall of black smoke, scurrying over to the Chevy. Luc slid in behind the wheel, clamped the seat belt across his chest and then looked at Veronica like a stern parent.

"Right," she said. "I know, I know, buckle up for

safety." She clicked the belt into place and he peeled out, zooming down the road to safety—or so she thought.

The instant the car hit high speed, Andrew Scott, hidden, coiled in the backseat, reared like a wild beast and struck. He looped a rope around Luc's neck and leaned back, trying to choke the life from his adversary.

The taut cord cut into Luc's windpipe and artery. Keeping one hand on the wheel, he scratched at the noose with the other, trying to claw himself free of the deadly snare. His nails raked his throat, lacerating the skin, but he couldn't tear himself free.

When Scott pounced, Veronica had screamed and recoiled in fear. Then, realizing that she was the only person in the car capable of freeing her companion, she struck back, her fingers curved like talons. Her fingernails tore into his face, carving long, bloody tracks on his cheeks. Scott hardly reacted at all, bearing down on his principal adversary. There would be plenty of time to deal with the woman when he had strangled Luc.

"You can't run from me this time," Scott growled through gritted teeth. "Traitor!"

The cord was cutting into Luc's neck, a ribbon of bright red blood welling over the rope. Veronica struck out with her fists, but her puny blows seemed to bounce off of Andrew Scott's hard body and head. One blow knocked his communication headset flying, but he continued to ignore her,

133

throwing all his weight behind his murderous attack on Luc.

The cord was so tight that the blood reaching Luc's brain had been reduced to the merest trickle. His vision was fogging and he felt light-headed. His skin had turned ash white, then gray, and was now a sickly slate blue. Soon he would pass out—and Scott would have won. There was only one thing he could do, one maneuver that would shake Scott from his deadly grasp—or kill them all.

The only weapon he had at hand was the car itself. He yanked the wheel, throwing the Chevy off the road and into the rough. The automobile jolted on the hard ground, streaking across the open country, headed directly for a pile of boulders, a heap of rocks standing no more than a few feet high. Luc could just make them out through his hazy eyes.

He stamped on the accelerator, and the car hit the stones at high speed, head-on. There was a sickening crash as the headlights blew out and the bumpers crumpled. For a second it seemed as if the force of impact would push the entire heavy V-6 engine back into the passenger compartment, crushing the riders in the front seat. But the weighty frame held firm, as the sheet metal of the hood buckled and folded back on itself, as if it were no stronger than a sheet of paper.

Locked in behind their seat belts, Veronica and Luc were held firmly at the moment of the collision, but Andrew Scott had no restraint on him whatsoever. The instant the Chevrolet smashed into the immovable barrier of boulders, he was pitched forward, flying over the front seat and smashing into the safety glass windshield. His body blew through the window like a human bullet, shattering it into thousands of jagged fragments, the sharp splinters lacerating his face and neck. He bounced once on the warped hood and landed hard on the jagged boulders. His head smacked into the unforgiving rock, and he lay sprawled, stunned by the force of his painful landing.

The rope was embedded in Luc's neck, cut into the skin. He snatched at it and tossed it aside, doubling over the steering wheel, coughing and hacking, trying to clear his bruised and constricted throat, forcing air into his lungs.

Dazed and almost unconscious, Scott was dimly aware that he had to rise from his rocky bed and confront his enemy once again. Accustomed as he was to the invulnerability of the Unisols, he tried to get up, but his bruised and broken body refused to respond. He shook his head like a boxer clearing his head after a particularly savage blow.

Luc recovered a few moments faster than Scott. The Chevrolet had stalled out when it hit the rocks, and he knew he had to get the engine fired up and out of there before Scott rejuvenated himself. He twisted the key in the ignition, and the engine turned over raggedly, the pistons groaning and kicking, faltering, refusing to catch.

Luc had forced himself to sit up, and was

beginning to struggle to his feet. The engine continued to wail, screaming at the rough treatment Luc was subjecting it to. He wrenched the key in the ignition as hard as he could, smashing his foot down on the gas, urging the battered engine to life. It was a race now, a tortuous contest between two nearly ruined machines—Scott and the Chevy—to see which could get running first.

The car won by a hair. The engine finally caught, turning over raggedly, black smoke billowing out of the exhaust pipe and from under the hood. Luc threw it into reverse, and the Chevy rattled backward and onto the roadway.

Scott was on his feet, watching the Chevy withdraw across the rough terrain. His tattered, bloody face, his savaged body—he looked like a vision from hell. As the car hit the highway and clattered away, he felt a hot surge of overpowering hate. He threw his head back like an animal and wailed, a powerful scream torn from his throat. It was more than just a hot howl of loathing; it was a vow, a war cry.

Chapter Nine

The fireball at the gas station was burning itself out now, but as far as Colonel Perry was concerned the catastrophe was far from over. The three burned Unisols were hideously damaged and the chance of saving them only fifty-fifty at best, and he could tell just by looking at Woodward's pessimistic face that his chief scientist on the Unisol project rated their chances as much lower.

He found it hard to believe that things could get much worse, but when Garth came hurrying out of the truck, a piece of paper in his hand, he discovered that when things went bad, they went *really* bad.

"I have a fax from headquarters, Colonel Perry," said Garth. He had already read it, and he stepped away from the operations commander, as if getting out of the path of a massive explosion.

Perry looked at the fax transmission, his face darkening as he read each word.

"Shit!" he roared. "Pack it up. We've been ordered back home. They're pulling the plug on this operation. Goddammit! Son of a bitch!"

Garth decided to play innocent. "Sir?"

"Change of plans," Colonel Perry yelled. "A change of plans and we're not included. We fucked up and they know it. Let's go. Everyone back in the truck."

Andrew Scott was walking back into the scene of devastation. Perry, still angry at his Unisol for *almost* disobeying orders at the beginning of the botched attack, turned on him.

"GR 13!"

Scott stopped and looked long and hard at the Unisol mission commander. Then, ignoring him, he turned and gazed over his shoulder, staring down the highway, as if he could still see Luc and Veronica although they had already disappeared in the vastness of the Nevada desert.

"GR 13! I'm talking to you."

Slowly, grudgingly, Scott turned to face his commander again.

"The mission is canceled," said Colonel Perry sharply. "Get back in the truck."

Scott did not respond. He didn't move a muscle. Perry, used to the instant obedience of the well-trained Universal Soldier, gaped at him, amazed.

"Are you listening to me?" he demanded. "Did you hear me, soldier?"

Scott was silent.

"GR 13! I said it's over! I said get in the truck. You will always obey orders, GR 13."

Very calmly, the Universal Soldier spoke. "I am not GR 13."

Colonel Perry could not quite believe his ears. "What? What did you say?"

"I said, I am not GR 13." He paused. "My name," he said almost reasonably, almost humanly, "is Sergeant Andrew Scott."

"Your what?" Perry was astonished.

"And as for this mission, Perry," Scott continued, "it is not over. It's just begun."

"GR 13, you better get your ass in gear or I'm gonna—" Sergeant Andrew Scott never found out just how horrible Colonel Perry's threat would be. Smoothly, in one motion, he drew his Colt .45 automatic and fired once, the bullet hitting Perry square in the right eye, throwing the colonel's body against the truck. He died in mid-heartbeat.

Andrew Scott holstered his pistol and walked toward the body, unsheathing his bowie knife as he went. There was almost a spring in his step.

The small team inside the truck was working feverishly, rushing to get the giant, sprawling vehicle ready for travel back to base and attending to the three stricken Universal Soldiers. The trio of burn victims had been hoisted into flotation tanks, vast vats filled with a concentrated dose of the coolant sprayed on their burning bodies during the height of the fire a few minutes before. The chemical was mixed with a restoring agent that stimulated new cell growth and strengthened the muscles that had been seared by the flames. A third drug stabilized the vital organs of the injured men, keeping the heart, lungs, eyes and brain steady and secure while the regeneration process took its course.

The three men were suspended in the tubs, plastic tubing plugged into their mouths and veins and floating around them like tentacles. Their charred skin sloughed off in sheets, black membranes scrolling off the incinerated bodies and sinking to the bottom of the tanks.

Garth and Woodward had suited up in protective clothing and were within the Unisol cooling unit, checking over the remaining soldiers. All of them showed some degree of damage from the combination of action and extreme temperatures— overheating that would impair their effectiveness the next time they were called into operation. A number of evil-looking stainless steel medical instruments lay fanned out on a metal table, ready for use if Woodward thought it necessary to perform any sudden surgery.

The Unisols were damaged but not severely, and secretly Woodward was relieved by the degree of maltreatment. He would have to work them over properly when they returned to their base, but for the time being they seemed stable enough for travel.

He spoke through his protective helmet, knowing that his voice would be picked up by the powerful microphones installed in the room.

"Colonel Perry, we are ready for you back at command. I have a preliminary report . . ."

He turned back to the Unisols, sitting immobile in their thrones, and continued to check them out. He shone a small flashlight in their eyes, checking the strength of their reflexes.

There was no answering call from Colonel Perry.

"Colonel Perry? Do you read?"

He turned Garth. "Where the hell is he?"

"Outside, I think. I didn't see him come back in."

"Colonel Perry? Copy please . . ."

"You're wasting your time."

Both Garth and Woodward looked up from their ministrations. Andrew Scott was standing over them, an eerie curl of condensation smoke spiraling off his body as his hot skin hit the freezing temperatures of the cooling chamber.

"GR 13! What are you talking about?" demanded Woodward. There was something different about the Unisol. Whatever it was, Garth and his fellow technician didn't like it.

"He can't hear you," said Andrew Scott. By way of explanation, he dumped two bloody ears onto the steel table, gore spilling out over the sterilized instruments.

Garth and Woodward jumped back, fear pulsing through their bodies.

"Jesus!" cried Garth.

Woodward managed to keep his horror somewhat under control. "What the hell are you playing at, GR 13?"

"I have relieved Colonel Perry of his command."

"You've done what? The hell you have, soldier!" All three men looked to see who had spoken.

Beyond the coolant chamber stood Lieutenant Sullivan. He was staring sternly through the glass. He may have been an expert at dealing with the press, but he was also a serving officer in the Special Forces. Sullivan was, in his own way, just as tough and no-nonsense an officer as Colonel Perry. He was also just as unscrupulous.

Andrew Scott looked coldly at the lieutenant and sneered. Then he sauntered out of the coolant chamber and faced him down. "I said, I have relieved Colonel Perry of his command. This operation is now under my control."

"GR 13," said Sullivan harshly, "you have your orders. This mission has been canceled by directive of your superiors. I order you to return to your place in the cooling chamber. Now!"

Andrew Scott smiled. In fact, he almost laughed. "Orders? I'm giving the orders from now on."

"What!? You are dead meat, soldier! When we get back to base I'm gonna—" Like his superior, Lieutenant Sullivan never got a chance to make good on his threat.

Scott whipped his automatic out of his holster like a Western gunslinger and fired a single bullet directly into Sullivan's heart. He fell back, slamming against the thick glass partition that separated the command center from the cooling chamber. Sullivan hit the window divider and then slid down to the floor, his path greased by a trail of blood.

Gun in hand, Scott turned to Garth and Woodward. He could see their terrified eyes behind the eyepieces of their protective helmets.

"Any questions?" he asked.

Woodward and Garth stared through their clear Plexiglas visors, the look on their faces sick and scared.

"I asked if there were any questions."

Garth shook his head.

Woodward wasn't quite so wise. "GR 13, I think you should consider the position you're in. If you think about it for a moment—"

Scott raised his gun, aiming it through the glass, directly at Woodward's forehead. "Maybe you should consider yours, Woodward."

The scientist's nerve failed him. He turned back to the Unisols still sitting in their assigned places, as dumb and as uncomplaining as farm animals.

Andrew Scott adjusted very well to command. "Medics," he ordered, "get my soldiers ready. We have a mission to complete."

Luc coaxed as much power as he could out of the battered Chevy, putting a good fifty miles between him and the Unisols before he brought the pummeled and windowless car to a halt in front of a roadside truck stop. He knew that if he went much farther, the much put-upon Chevrolet would, like a Unisol, overheat and shut down.

Luc parked in the dusty lot in front of the

restaurant, turning off the hot engine, hoping that he'd be able to get the motor started again. It was important. If he was sure of one thing—and he wasn't sure of much—he knew that they would be running again. The Unisol command wouldn't leave them alone. Not until Veronica was dead and Luc Devreux was brought back into the Universal Soldier fold and neutralized.

Veronica opened the door of the car and stretched, trying to calm herself down and take stock of the situation. It was not, she realized, a terribly encouraging picture. Huey was dead—how long ago that incident seemed—and she had been framed for the murder and tarred as a drug dealer to boot. There was a force of cold, brutal killers on her trail, destroying everything in their path to get to her, and her only protection was some kind of weird automaton who had a number instead of a name and no personal history he could remember—except that he had been dead once.

Given the pickle she was in, it was hard to remember what the real world was like, that ordinary life was still going on. She looked around her. The sun was shining in a blue sky. Kids were playing in the parking lot and people were eating in the truck stop. Huge sixteen-wheel truck rigs were parked haphazardly all over the lot. Periodically, another truck zoomed by on the highway, air horn blowing in salute to the truckers climbing out of their cabs and making for the restaurant. It was a scene Veronica had seen a thousand times before, but now, in the light of all she had been through in the past twenty-four hours, the everydayness seemed bizarre.

The normality of life around her made Veronica's circumstances seem that much more desperate and strange. It was not the brightest, most cheering situation she had ever been in. But she was in it and she was going to get herself out of it.

She retrieved the file folders and other documents she and Luc had stolen from the Unisol command truck, and together they lugged them into the diner.

It was a typical roadside truck stop diner—a couple of booths upholstered in worn red Naugahyde, a jukebox full of Waylon and Willie, a bar, and an old pool table in the corner. Given that they were in Nevada, there were the requisite three or four slot machines standing here and there, waiting for suckers and their silver dollars.

Most of the people in the restaurant were truckers, big men, good ol' boys shoveling food into their mouths. Chili, steak and eggs, huge sandwiches and burgers—the smell of hot grease and meat made Luc Devreux realize how hungry he was.

But food didn't seem to be on Veronica's mind. She ordered a cup of coffee and settled in a booth, spreading the purloined documents out on the table in front of her. She shook a cigarette out of the pack, lit it and studied the papers, her brow knit in concentration. Luc didn't seem interested in them at all. He picked up the cigarette pack and studied it.

It only took a moment or two for Veronica to realize that she was in way over her head—she couldn't make heads or tails of the technical documents.

She exhaled a stream of smoke heavily, frustrated. "I feel like I'm back in high school, in physics class or something. You know?"

Luc looked at her blankly, uncomprehending.

"No," she said, shaking her head, "I guess you wouldn't. Stupid question . . . This stuff is way too technical for me, but from what I can gather, whatever they did to you, they did it on a genetic level." The term "genetic engineering" shot into her mind. It was one of those phrases that she heard all the time but never paid any attention to. She recalled that her own news organization, CNA, had done a story on it recently, and she hadn't even bothered to watch it. Now, she wished she had.

"I don't suppose you could shed any light on this? You don't remember *anything*?"

Luc put down the pack of cigarettes and plucked the smoke out of her mouth. "The surgeon general has determined that cigarette smoking can be hazardous to your health," he said primly.

Veronica glared at him and snatched back the cigarette. "Yeah? Don't believe everything you read. I should know. I write it."

He picked up the cigarette pack and crushed it in his hard hand.

"What the hell are you doing?"

"Preventing you from damaging your health."

She slammed the folder shut, angry now. "Now listen, there are a bunch of guys with more guns than the army chasing us. Right now *they're* the health hazard. I'll worry about smoking when things are a little less dangerous, okay?"

The waitress had come up to the table, handing them menus and placing two glasses of water in front of them, cutting off Veronica's anger.

"Would you like to order?"

Veronica tossed her menu aside. The waitress was looking at her suspiciously, as if she might have seen her someplace before, like on television. Paranoid now, Veronica wanted to get rid of the waitress as quickly as possible. No time to study the menu. "Bring us . . . uh, bring us two of your specials."

"Two specials." The waitress noted their order, then struck her pencil back behind her ear. "Got it."

Veronica glared at Luc, still irate at the treatment meted out to her cigarettes. As she turned back to the folders, she wondered if the truck stop had a cigarette machine.

"I was only trying to help you," said Luc contritely.

"Well, I'm trying to help *you*." She scanned one of the documents intently. They keep on referring to a doctor. Dr. Christopher Gregor. Do you recognize that name?"

Deep in his brain, the name seemed familiar, but he couldn't place it exactly. "I'm not sure . . ."

Veronica flipped through the pages quickly, her eyes running down the columns of text, looking for more on the mysterious Dr. Gregor. "I know I saw a number somewhere here . . . Where is that damn thing . . ."

"Do you think he can help me?"

"I don't know . . . It's worth a shot. We're not going to get out of this thing alone, that's for sure."

She continued to read. Luc stared at her, really looking at her for the first time. There was no denying her prettiness—even on the run, without sleep and having gone through twenty-four hours of hell, she was lovely. But the intensity of Luc's gaze was due to more than her beauty.

She was studying the papers, but she was aware of his scrutiny, and she shifted uncomfortably, trying to concentrate on the text. Finally, she looked up.

"What? What's on your mind?"

"I was confused . . ."

"Yeah, you and me both."

"I was wondering why you are doing this for me."

Veronica turned back to the papers. "I'm not doing it for you. I'm doing it for me . . ."

"For you?" asked Luc sadly.

"Yeah. You may not realize it yet, but you are

one hell of a story. But don't worry. When the truth comes out, they'll make you a hero. They will probably throw a parade in your honor. Me, they'll frame for murder and toss in jail and throw away the key. Unless we get the hell out of this mess."

"We'll get out," he assured her.

But she wasn't listening. Hand-written at the bottom of one of the dense pages was a note.

"Here it is," she said, excited by her discovery. "C.G. (505) KL5-8826. C.G.—that must stand for Christopher Gregor. Let's check it out." She jumped up and dug in her purse for change. "I'm going to go find a phone. I'll be right back."

She bolted from the table just as the waitress arrived with their food. "Two specials," she said, putting down huge plates of barbecued beef accompanied by mounds of french fries and onion rings.

Methodically, Luc began eating, stuffing food into his mouth quickly, chewing and swallowing, never stopping, systematically devouring everything on his plate. In a matter of minutes the platter was cleaned. He sat still for a moment, looking at Veronica's plate of steaming food. He glanced over his shoulder and saw her in the glass-enclosed booth talking animatedly. She showed no signs of returning. It would, he decided, be a shame to waste the food. He traded plates with her and began eating Veronica's portion. He felt a little guilty, but what could he do? He was hungry.

• • •

In the Unisol command vehicle, Woodward and Garth were doing their best to fight their fears and revive the three damaged soldiers. They were in the chest of one of the injured soldiers, leaning over, deep in his body like mechanics working under the hood of an automobile. They tried to concentrate on their grisly task, but they kept shooting nervous glances at Sergeant Andrew Scott. The former Unisol was pacing back and forth in the command center, agitated and anxious to get out on the road again. There was nothing he could do until the force was up to strength.

Suddenly, he stopped and snatched up a huge syringe that lay on the stainless steel table. The glass cylinder was filled with a dark blue liquid. He aimed the long, sharp needle at his heart like a dagger and jabbed the keen spike deep into his chest, thrusting the shaft into his heart.

He didn't wince, and he didn't hesitate to plunge the hammer of the syringe, forcing the liquid into his bloodstream.

Garth, squeamish as usual about needles, looked away. "What the hell is he doing?"

Woodward looked worried and bit his lip. "He's overloading on muscle enhancers. He's making himself stronger."

Scott's already huge muscles seemed to grow under his skin, flexing and spasming, inflating as if attached to a pump. Scott looked down at his brawny chest and smiled, a satisfied snarl breaking from his lips.

Garth quaked at the sight. "That's just great. That's all we need—a stronger version of him."

"We have to do something—and fast," said Woodward. "He's going to go out of control and get us all killed."

"Any bright ideas?"

Woodward nodded. "Something that might work. Anyway, I hope it does."

"That makes two of us."

Woodward walked over to Andrew Scott. He was bent over the stainless steel table, busy working on something, engrossed in the task at hand.

"Sergeant Scott," Woodward said, his voice low and respectful, as if he accepted the young Unisol as the legitimate leader of the unit. "May I have a word with you?"

Scott smiled evilly. He had daubed his face with war paint, and he looked meaner and more brutal than he ever had. He showed the scientist the object of his labors. It was a necklace of ears, two from Perry and two from Lieutenant Sullivan, strung on a piece of wire. "I'm all *ears*," he said with a sneer. He chuckled as he tied the grisly souvenir around his neck.

Woodward fought his revulsion, swallowing hard and nervously.

"Look at your thermal monitor. It's registering hot."

Scott raised his arm and looked at the chronometer on his wrist. The light in the center of the dial was pulsing a lemon yellow.

"Uh-oh, nap time," said Scott.

"You better take your seat in the cooling chamber."

"Right." Scott walked back into the frigid room, taking his place among the other Unisols.

Garth freaked out. He was in the command center, watching Scott nervously. "Why the hell did you do that?" he whispered to Woodward harshly. "Are you nuts? Why did you tell him he was overheating? He would have shut down and we would've been in the clear."

"There's no telling what he would have done. He's not performing to specification as it is. Besides, it takes ninety minutes for one of these things to overheat and shut down. He could have killed us all in that time. This way is better."

"What are you going to do?"

"I'm going to quadruple his serum. Kill him."

"How the hell are you going to do that?" Garth whispered back urgently. "The injector is preset. You have to go in there to change it."

"That's exactly what I'm going to do. When he's ready, I'll give you a signal, you turn up the juice and I'll hit the injection device on the arm of the chair."

Woodward started toward the cooling chamber, but Garth pulled him back. "I always work in the chamber," he said. "You go in there and he'll suspect. I'll do it."

Before Woodward could protest, Garth pushed

by him. Woodward watched his younger colleague nervously and then turned back to the control panel, busying himself but ready to act on Garth's signal.

Garth tried to act nonchalant, casually going from soldier to soldier, checking and rechecking their meter settings. When he got to Scott, he was intensely aware of the berserk soldier's eyes on him. Just as Garth reached for the control on the injection device, Scott's hand whipped out and grabbed him by the wrist.

Scott jumped up and grabbed Garth by the throat, strangling him through the heavy material of the coolant suit. "Is there a problem, Medic?" he said through gritted teeth.

"The injection device," Garth managed to gasp, through Scott's murderous choke hold. "I was going to fix it."

"Is it broken?" Scott didn't really care about the answer. His grip tightened and closed Garth's throat tight. "I guess there's only one way to find out . . ."

Scott tore the helmet off Garth's head and threw the hapless man into his chair, putting his foot on Garth's chest, pinning him to the chair.

Garth whimpered and tried to free himself, but his head was secure in the headrest. Scott jabbed the injection button.

"No!" screamed Garth, his voice cracking in the icy air. "Please! Please don't!"

Woodward threw his body against the glass, flattening himself there. "Stop! You'll kill him!"

The metal claw of the injection apparatus seized Garth's head, holding it firm. The needle shot into the back of his head, skewering his brain. His death howl was loud and shrill.

When the waitress returned to remove the wreckage of the two plates of food, she flipped out her order pad. "Can I get you anything else? Coffee? Dessert?"

Luc studied the menu. "I'd like two orders of meat loaf."

She looked at him warily. Meat loaf was not generally considered dessert in this place. "Two meat loaf," she repeated, jotting it down. "Anything else?"

"A club sandwich, an order of pork chops, string beans, salad, soup and this—" He pointed to some unfamiliar, unpronounceable words on the menu.

"Huevos rancheros?"

"That's right."

"Anything else?"

"A bowl of chili."

"You got quite an appetite, don'cha?"

"Yes," said Luc.

In the phone booth on the far side of the dining room, Veronica was oblivious to the gargantuan meal being consumed at her table.

She was more concerned with getting Charles Hoover, her former employer and field producer, to believe her story. He was steadfastly resisting her version of events, and her anger was about to go ballistic.

Hearing her voice on the phone and listening to her crazy story about a unit of indestructible, government-operated and trained soldiers destroying and killing without remorse in a remote part of the Southwest, he was even more inclined to believe the police version of events: that Veronica, despondent over being fired by CNA, had flipped out on drugs and murdered Huey. He told her so, too.

"How the hell can you believe that?" she shouted down the line. "It's *me*, Charles. You know me; I would never do anything like that. You've just fallen into a government disinformation trap. You're a newsman! I can't believe it!"

All this sounded like the typical paranoid ravings of a drug abuser. "Ronnie, why don't you tell me where you are?" he said soothingly. "I can help you."

"The hell with that, Charles. I was set up! *Those* bastards killed Huey and I'm not going to let them get away with it. Do you hear me?"

"You're sick, Ronnie. Turn yourself in and get help. Do yourself a favor. This kind of behavior is just making things harder on yourself."

Veronica tried a different tack. She hoped that she would be able to play on Charles's constant desire for the Big Story, something that would blow the network and cable competition out of the water. "I've got a major lead here. This story is very big, Charles, the biggest story of *my* career, *your* career."

The big story angle did nothing to convince her

155

former employer of her sanity. In fact, it had quite the opposite effect. As far as Charles was concerned, she was really raving now. "Ronnie," he pleaded, "get help." He put down the phone.

For a second, she couldn't quite believe that he had hung up on her. "Charles?" she shouted. "Charles, for God's sake!" She slammed the receiver down on the cradle. "Shit!"

She stood in the phone booth, attempting to quell her fiery anger. Had she looked over her shoulder, she would have seen a constant stream of waitresses ferrying plate after plate of food to Luc. His consumption was beginning to catch the attention of the patrons, including a couple of truckers at the counter of the diner. The cooks and the busboys were coming out of the kitchen to gawk at Luc's prodigious consumption of food.

As one of the waitresses delivered a steaming plate of fried chicken to the table, she looked at Luc and shook her head. "Amazing. It's just amazing you don't have a weight problem, son."

Luc attacked the chicken as if it were the first food he had seen in days. "I am very active," he said between giant bites.

"I'll bet you are, darlin'."

Luc turned back to his food.

"I'm kinda 'fraid to ask," said the waitress, "but will there be anything else?"

"Steak and eggs," he said, "a bacon, lettuce and tomato sandwich and chicken fried steak."

"Mashed potatoes with that?"

"Yes, please."

"You know," said the waitress, "I had a feeling you'd say that."

Veronica scrabbled through the pages of the loose-leaf binder, looking for the number of the mysterious Dr. Christopher Gregor. She dialed quickly and got a response almost immediately— the long, whiny beep of a fax machine answering her call. "Shit!" So far, it had not been a good day.

The truckers who had been watching Luc from the counter of the diner decided that they might be able to have a little fun at his expense. The plate of steak and eggs and the chicken fried steak were sitting in the service hatch waiting for one of the overworked waitresses to pick them up and deliver them to Luc.

One of the men elbowed his buddy in the ribs. "You know, I think he might need some extra seasoning." The trucker unscrewed the top from a full bottle of Tabasco sauce and poured the red liquid fire all over the steak and eggs, emptying it to the last drop. "Let's see what that does to his appetite," he said with a broad wink. His companion howled with laughter.

One of the waitresses grabbed the plate and placed it before Luc. He dove into the food, gobbling, unfazed by the hot sauce. The truckers stared, flabbergasted.

"I don't believe it," said the prankster.

"Something pretty screwy about that boy," added the other trucker.

"I shoulda put two bottles on it."

Luc had consumed close to two hundred dollars'

worth of food, and the waitresses were beginning to get a little worried about the rising bill and whether or not he would be able to put a nice fat tip on top of it.

Luc munched on his bacon, lettuce and tomato sandwich, perusing the menu for the next wave of nourishment. The spare ribs caught his eye. "I'll have—"

"Look," said the waitress, cutting him off, "before I get you another thing I want to know if you're good for it. You're running up a hell of a check here, mister."

"Good for it?" asked Luc, confused by the question. "What does that mean?"

"It means, do you have any money?"

"Money?"

"You know . . . money." She rubbed her thumb across her finger tips. "Money? Dollars? Moola?" She had noted his accent and wondered if he were Mexican—after all the border wasn't all that far away. Course, he didn't know how to pronounce "huevos rancheros," but she changed languages anyway. "You know, *dinero?*"

It had never occurred to Luc that he was going to have to pay for all this. "I'm sorry . . . ," he said.

The waitress rolled her eyes. "I knew it. I just knew it all along."

"Perhaps—" began Luc.

"Perhaps what? Perhaps you'll wash dishes? No way." She turned and, hands on hips, yelled into the kitchen. "Hank! We got ourselves a deadbeat back here!" She had a voice as strident and as penetrating as that of a hog caller.

Her shrill words got an immediate response. The door of the kitchen slammed open and the cook emerged. He was a huge man, dressed in grimy white pants, a torn-up T-shirt and a dirty apron. He did not look pleased by what he had heard.

"What? What did you say?" he demanded of the waitress.

She jerked a thumb at Luc. "He can't pay."

The cook started walking over to Luc, who was finishing his sandwich. "Hey, punk," shouted Hank the cook, "you got any idea how long I slaved making all that slop?"

Luc nodded appreciatively. "The food is really good. I congratulate you."

The truckers at the bar, riveted by the scene before them, laughed and hooted. "Hey, Hank," shouted one of them. "He *congratulates* you."

"That's right nice of you," said Hank affably. Then he reached down and yanked Luc to his feet. Face-to-face like that, it was apparent that the cook was bigger and brawnier than Luc. He was taller too, and towered over him. "You like the food?" he said, holding Luc tightly by the front of his uniform.

"Yes," Luc repeated, "it is very good. Really."

"Fuckin' A, it's really good. Question is, how the hell are you gonna pay for it?"

Luc considered this for a moment, raising half of his BLT to his mouth. Before he could bite down on it, though, Hank slapped it away, the sandwich flying across the room.

"I don't want any trouble," said Luc.

"Well, for someone who don't want any trouble, you are about neck deep in it. Punk."

Luc tried to be as sincere as possible, sure he could reason with the man. "I do not want to hurt you."

Hank laughed. "*You*? Hurt *me*?" He turned to the truckers at the counter. "You hear that, boys? He says he doesn't want to hurt me. Can you beat that?"

"Ooooh, Hank, you be careful there. You should be scared."

"Oh, I am . . . I *am*." The cook turned back to face Luc, launching a hairy fist at him, throwing his full weight behind the blow.

It was a heavy punch with a lot of force built into it, but it was slow and the cook was a flat-footed brawler, more concerned with taking his opponents out with a single, thundering punch. Luc was way ahead of him. He saw the punch coming a mile or two off, and still anxious to avoid a full-scale fight, he sidestepped the blow and merely deflected it with an open-palm punch. But he simply didn't know his own strength—his already awesome power had been pumped up and super-charged by the giant meal he had just consumed. Even a light tap sent the cook flying.

Hank slammed into the jukebox, his fist shattering the glass. He hit the machine with such force that the mechanism sparked and a record dropped onto the turntable. Waylon Jennings's voice filled the room, advising mothers not to let their babies grow up to be cowboys. No one paid too much attention to his counsel.

This was getting serious now. The three truckers, seeing Hank go down in a shower of glass and music, decided that it was time they got involved. Two of them didn't hesitate. They charged Luc simultaneously, but neither of them got any closer than Luc would allow. He slammed one with a hard, driving side kick, hurling him across the room. He hit the felt of the pool table, sliding along the fairway, his head cracking into the balls neatly racked in a triangle at one end. His hard skull acted as a pretty good cue ball—he sunk a couple of the object balls in the side and back pockets, but the other people in the room were too busy to notice the nice break.

The second trucker went down in a flurry of fast blows, giving Luc ample time to grab a carton of milk from the counter. He popped it open and drank it down in a gulp or two. He was busy drinking when the third trucker slammed a chair over his head, splintering it. If the man had expected his opponent to go down under the force of such a mighty blow, he was disappointed. Luc turned slowly, as if the smack with a hardwood chair had been a discreet tap on his shoulder meant to get his attention and nothing more. He finished the milk, burped and wiped the big milk moustache off his upper lip.

"Milk," he said, "it does a body good."

"Yeah? Well try this." The man lowered his shoulder and with a roar charged at Luc like an onrushing bull. Luc sidestepped the attack like a skilled matador, caught the man by the collar of his shirt and the seat of his pants and tossed him onto the bar. The guy slid along the counter, cake stands and sugar bowls and plates of food flying. He slammed into the mirrored back wall of the diner, his head cracking the thick glass and bringing down shelf after shelf of bottles.

To his delight, Luc noticed that there was still half a sandwich untouched on his plate. He picked it up and began munching contentedly . . .

Veronica was just wrapping up her phone call. She had called directory assistance for the 505 area code.

"Yes, a local number, Operator, prefix KL5. Dr. Christopher Gregor."

"I have a Gregor, C.," the operator reported, "but it's not a residence. It's a hospital."

"Must be the same guy," said Veronica.

"The Veterans Administration Hospital. That's in Clinton."

"And where's Clinton?"

"That would be near Vaughn, ma'am."

Veronica felt a little stupid asking the next question. "Uh, and what state would that be?"

There was the tiniest pause before the operator answered. It was, she seemed to be thinking, a little early in the day for the crazy calls. "New Mexico, ma'am."

"Great. Thank you." Veronica hung up and

walked back into the diner. She surveyed the devastation and looked at Luc, still chewing placidly, like a ruminant.

The waitress pounced on her the instant she appeared. "He with you?"

"Uh . . . yeah."

The waitress whipped a check out of her order book. "Your bill."

She had tacked an extra thousand bucks onto the food bill to cover the damage. Veronica read the numbers and blanched.

"Do you, by any chance, take plastic?"

Luc looked up from his food and, for the first time, smiled at her. She smiled back.

A few minutes later, the battered Chevy was back on the road and Veronica was in debt to the tune of twelve hundred bucks. But that was okay—the smile had been worth the price.

Chapter Ten

They had a long way to go—they were in central Nevada and they had to get to New Mexico, and that meant that there was a lot of Arizona between them and their destination. They drove all day, stopping only for gas. They couldn't drive in a straight line, taking the most direct route from point A to B. Despite all the confusion, it had never left Veronica's mind that she was wanted for murder, so they avoided built-up areas, cities and towns where the news of Huey's death might have been widely disseminated and the cops on the lookout for her.

They had to avoid Las Vegas and the heavily patrolled area around the Grand Canyon, right on the Nevada-Arizona line. They cut deep to the south, through the Mojave Desert, adding hundreds of miles to their already long journey. Glendale, Scottsdale, Phoenix and Tucson were also danger spots, so they had to head through another desert, the Sonoran, bumping along on slow two-lane blacktops, instead of making good time on the big super-highways.

By nightfall, they were in eastern Arizona, making slow headway in the mountains around Morenci and Gillis. By the time the stars came out and the moon rose, Veronica was so exhausted, drained by the stress and strain of the last two days, that she burrowed down in the front seat of the Chevy and fell asleep. It was cold in the mountains, and she shivered as the chilly air coursed through the gaping hole where the front windshield used to be.

Luc welcomed the onrushing, cold mountain air. He tore open his uniform tunic and let the blasting wind flow over him, cooling him down. From time to time he looked over at Veronica, sleeping fitfully at his side. There was a tenderness in his gaze that no one in his recent past—Perry, Woodward, Garth, even Andrew Scott—would have recognized. This, although he didn't realize it, was a long-dormant emotion stirring within him: love.

They skirted Albuquerque, swung south to Lordsburg and Cookes Peak, then headed north for the central part of the state. They hit the small town of Vaughn at daybreak and were on the outskirts of Clinton just as the sun came up over the horizon. Luc parked the broken-down Chevrolet on the edge of town and waited an hour or two for the little settlement to awake.

Veronica dozed for another few minutes, then woke with a start, the stillness of the car, in contrast to the rattling ride of the last day and night, pulling her from unconsciousness. Instantly, she was on her guard.

"What? What happened?" She sat up and rubbed her eyes.

"Nothing. We're there. There's nothing to worry about."

She was working her shoulders, swiveling her upper body. Her muscles seemed to have seized up overnight, and she felt achy and stiff.

"That's easy for you to say." She massaged her shoulders and lower back, trying to work out the kinks. "Jesus, am I tired . . ."

"You can sleep a little longer," he said.

"No." She checked her watch. "Seven-thirty. Hospitals wake up early. Let's go find Dr. Gregor and get this thing over with."

Luc nodded and coaxed the car back to life.

It wasn't hard to find the hospital—it was probably the largest building in the little town— and they rolled through the gates, with no one making a move to stop them.

The Clinton Veterans Administration Hospital was a large collection of buildings, some of them solid brick, others nothing more than prefabricated houses and Quonset huts. It looked like an army camp and it looked old—as if it had been built during the Second World War, much of it thrown up quickly, temporary housing for the great influx of wounded soldiers coming from the Pacific theater. Temporary became permanent, and the place was never closed down or renovated.

The main administration building was one of the more solid structures on the hospital grounds. The car rolled to a halt in front of it, and Luc and Veronica both stared at the front door.

"Well," said Veronica finally, "I guess this is the place to start."

She opened her door and he opened his. She put out a hand to stop him. "No. You wait here. I'll be right back. If he's there, I'll come and get you. Stay with the car. I might come out of there running."

The plan made sense, but he was nervous sitting in the car. He felt exposed, alone, uncomfortable in his vulnerable position—feelings that were as foreign to him as love and tenderness. He scanned the area. As time passed, people emerged from the various buildings. Doctors and nurses bustled by, stethoscopes draped around their necks; orderlies walked by trundling gurneys or medical equipment or oxygen tanks.

Patients limped from building to building. Luc looked curiously at them. They were middle-aged men in army fatigues; one of them sat in a wheelchair pushed by a nurse. He was about a hundred yards off, but Luc's keen enhanced eyesight picked up the American flag pin on the old soldier's lapel. An empty flap of trouser leg was pinned at his waist, and both sleeves of his olive-drab fatigue shirt were vacant.

Luc was puzzled—he had seen wounds just like

that in Vietnam. Multiple amputees were usually victims of Vietcong antipersonnel mines, cleverly concealed explosive devices that were spring-loaded. When a soldier's boot hit one, it tripped and jumped to about waist height, discharging a curtain of jagged metal that cut through bone and flesh, lopping off limbs like flower stalks. But the vet looked so *old*. He *couldn't* have been in 'Nam.

Other veterans stumped by. It seemed that the Clinton VA Hospital specialized in wounds involving the loss of limbs. Virtually every man Luc saw was missing an arm, a leg, a foot, a hand. They walked on crutches or were pushed in wheelchairs, another vet or a nurse behind.

He jumped when he heard Veronica's voice. "He's here," she said, throwing herself into the car. "He hasn't come on duty yet, but he lives in a house right here on hospital grounds. Let's go."

Luc started the car and drove out of the parking lot slowly, watching the disabled veterans in the rearview mirror. There was something about the sight that disturbed him—and yet, he couldn't take his eyes off the damaged, dismembered men.

Dr. Gregor's house was a neat, white two-story Colonial clapboard house with green shutters, identical to the houses on either side. Veronica looked at the house for a moment before getting out of the car. There was absolutely nothing threatening about the trim little building, but she felt a cold tremor of fear as she stared at it: either they were about to make their first step toward getting out of this mess, or they were walking into a trap that would end their lives.

"Well . . . ," she said, "here goes."

They stood on the front step and rang the doorbell, which chimed deep in the house. A moment later, a young woman dressed like a maid answered the door.

"Can I help you?" She had a slight accent and the coloring of a Mexican.

"We'd like to talk to Dr. Gregor," Veronica said.

The maid looked nervously at Luc. "Do you have an appointment?"

Veronica hesitated a moment and then lied. "Yes," she said. "We are expected." She sincerely hoped they weren't expected—that would ruin everything.

"Follow me, please." The maid led them into the house. The rooms were beautifully decorated with antique pieces of furniture, the old brown wood of which was buffed to a high shine. There were paintings on the paneled walls—old landscapes and portraits in heavy, ornate gilt frames. It was certainly a surprise to find such a well-appointed and tastefully decorated house on the grounds of an army hospital in the middle of New Mexico. It was as if they had stepped out of the desert and into a London club or a Parisian *hôtel particulier*. Plainly, Dr. Gregor was a man of breeding and taste.

The maid led them into a book-lined study in the rear of the house. "Please wait here," she said. Veronica surveyed the bookcases and the expanse of mahogany desk. There was a silver box on the desk, and she opened it and then closed it, looking disappointed.

"What are you doing?"

"I'm looking for a cigarette."

"In a *doctor's* office?"

Veronica shrugged. "No, I guess not . . . But I tell you, I'd kill for a cigarette right now."

Luc looked puzzled. As one who had been trained to kill, swiftly and efficiently, it was not a word he would have used so lightly. "Why would you *kill* someone for a cigarette."

"It's just an expression. It's a figure of speech. I wouldn't actually *kill* someone . . ." She thought about the craving for nicotine that was nagging her nerves. "On second thought, I wouldn't actually kill, but I mean, I'd *hurt* them real bad, but kill them? No."

Luc had not quite developed a sense of humor. He had lost interest in her answer when she said she wouldn't actually *kill*—that was all he needed to hear—so he walked to the large windows and looked out.

A tall man with graying hair was in the backyard, pushing a young Mexican boy in a swing set. His back was to the house and Luc could not see his face, but it was easy to tell that he was being very playful with the gleeful boy, that he enjoyed pushing the child as much as the boy enjoyed being pushed.

The maid walked over and spoke to him. The man nodded and stopped propelling the swing. He turned toward the house, and for the first time Luc saw Dr. Christopher Gregor's face. The instant he saw the creased old face, a painful flash of memories shot through his mind.

Fine lines of sweat broke out on Luc Devreux's forehead and upper lip. In his mind he heard screams—his own screams—and he saw projected in his mind his own broken body, tethered to an operating table by leather straps. There was blood everywhere, lengths of bone and grisly pieces of tendon and muscle. The surgical instruments lay scattered in puddles of blood on steel trays.

Dr. Christopher Gregor was clear in Luc's mind, younger than he appeared to be now. His full head of hair was black, his skin tighter on his face. The doctor was standing over him, his green surgical scrubs black with blood. "You're going to be fine, Luc. Luc . . . ," he murmured.

The voice wavered and bent, the sound changing, echoing in his mind. The word remained the same, but the voice speaking it changed in tone and tenor. It was a woman's voice now, an accented voice, soft and gentle. The horrific scene of the operating theater vanished, and Luc saw a house, a farmhouse set in a green field, with a lazy brook curling somewhere in the middle distance. Far off, beyond the field, was a stand of evergreens.

"Luc . . . ," the woman called. "Luc. *Ou est tu? Tiens! Viens ici!*"

As if watching an old, grainy film of his own

life, he saw himself at ten years old, a little boy running in the fields, running toward the house, a man seated on the porch, rocking in a porch swing, the woman standing next to him. The boy was smiling brightly . . .

"Luc?" The voice was near at hand now. "Luc? Can you hear me?"

Luc's eyes snapped open. He was lying on the leather chesterfield couch in Dr. Gregor's office, the man leaning over him. Luc had no idea how he had come to be lying on the couch—he had no recollection of his collapse—and he was bathed in a great wave of sweat, the telltale sign of overheating. He started violently to see Christopher Gregor so close. Sweating and pale, Luc was totally disoriented, and he called out to the only person he could trust.

"Veronica?"

She leaned down and put her arm around his neck. "It's okay," she whispered calmly. "I'm right here."

He turned to her, his eyes scanning her as if he could somehow find the relief from his torment in her placid face. "I saw it . . ."

"Saw what?"

"I remember . . . I saw home . . ."

"Rest," said Veronica.

The temperature gauge on his wrist started to beep, flashing yellow, then changing quickly to red. Slowly, Luc sunk into unconsciousness, battling it all the way, unwilling to pass out, trying to

173

stay awake and keep hold of the vision he had just experienced. But his body overcame his will.

"Quickly," said Dr. Gregor. "We have to get him to the bathroom. We have to cover him with—"

"I know," said Veronica, "ice. He needs ice."

By dark the night before, the diner that Luc had trashed without breaking a sweat had gotten itself more or less back in working order. It was not the first time there had been a bar fight there, and Hank the cook had made more than one trip to a doctor to get sewn up after being decked by a patron.

The truckers that Luc had beat up had departed, painfully climbing into their rigs and hitting the road more or less on schedule. Their places at the bar had been taken by truck drivers not all that different in outlook and attitude to the guys who had occupied the bar stools earlier that day.

The only difference was that there were more of them—the trucks were parked in the lot for the night. The drivers would eat and drink in the truck stop, then climb up into the cabs of their rigs to digest the heavy fried food and sleep off the beer before hitting the road the next morning.

But the night was young yet. Big sixteen-wheel rigs were pulling up, and their drivers were getting down and stretching, greeting the guys they knew on the big haul lines. Music was drifting out of the roadhouse, and some of the men had come outside to drink beer out of long-neck bottles and enjoy the warm night air.

Conversation came to an abrupt halt as the Unisol truck came grinding up the highway. The men clustered around the diner were something of connoisseurs of trucks, and as they stared into the bright lights, not one of them could say that they had seen a sight quite like this before in their lives.

Their jaws dropped and they gaped; the beer bottles stopped halfway to their open mouths. The Unisol command truck thundered into the parking lot, pulling in next to the other trucks, but dwarfing the giant Macks and Peterbilt rigs already parked there.

"What the hell is that?" gasped the first trucker to regain the power of speech.

"Looks military," said his companion. "Would you look at the size of that mother."

The sliding door of the Unisol command truck swept open, and Andrew Scott emerged, his face painted, a wild look in his eye. He looked bigger than he had ever been before, the muscle-building stimulant he had ingested having kicked in. As he stood on the top step of the truck, the sides of the vehicle began expanding in a great hydraulic burst of power, cracking into the side of one of the sixteen wheelers, destroying the mirror-like finish and bursting a big, deep dent in its flank.

Scott strode up to the assembled truckers. "I'm looking for a deserter. He's traveling with a prisoner of war. A woman."

"A woman POW?" said one of the men. "Since when did we go to war?"

Scott turned and glared at the man, who shrunk back under the force of his malevolent gaze. "Sorry I asked," the man mumbled.

"Who has seen them?" growled Andrew Scott.

"Hey!" A bearded trucker was running out of the diner. "Look what you did to my truck." He stopped and looked at the buckled side of his vehicle, surveying the damage. Then he sprinted over to Scott. "My truck! You fucked up my truck, asshole." He thrust himself up, in close to Scott's face. "You're gonna pay for that, you mother-fucker."

Scott hardly looked at the man. He swatted him away with his beefy forearm, dispatching the burly driver as if he were no more threatening a foe than a playful puppy. There was incredible force behind the blow, however. Scott caught the man under the chin, picked him up and sent him sailing over a car parked by the door of the diner. He landed heavily, slamming into a garbage can.

Scott turned back to the truckers. He had already forgotten the bearded man. "The people I am looking for are in a white Chevy, no front or rear window."

No one spoke; they simply stared at this murderous apparition. Two of them were helping the bearded man to his feet, dusting him off.

"Hey," shouted one of the truckers. "What the hell planet you from, Tonto?"

Like a piece of heavy artillery locking on its

target, Scott turned to face the man. Then he started walking toward him slowly.

"Oh shit . . . ," said the trucker.

Inside the Unisol truck, Woodward looked away from the monitor bringing him the scene from outside the vehicle. Scott had gotten hold of one of the truckers and was pounding him with his big fist, hammering him again and again, methodically beating his hapless victim to a pulp.

Woodward closed his eyes and thought for a moment. With Scott outside the van, he knew the time to act and to act decisively had come. The injured Unisols were still in the regeneration tanks, their charred, blackened skin lying at the bottom of the pools. New pink skin was growing rapidly. Not only would the three men pull through, but before long they would be fit and ready for action. The rest of the Unisols sat in the cooling chamber, waiting to be activated.

Now was the time. "If you cannot stay cool," Woodward said aloud to himself, "you cannot stay alive." He sat at the controls of the regeneration tanks and twisted the temperature dials, raising the temperature up to zero. Almost instantly, the muscles in the bodies of the three healing Unisols spasmed. Their eyes opened wide; they were astonished to be experiencing something they had never known existed—death. All at once, the heart monitor lines on the screens flattened.

Woodward looked to the video monitors and saw that Scott had dropped his victim and decked another, kicking him in the ribs. Over the loudspeakers came the sickening sounds of bones shattering and cartilage parting.

Seeing that Andrew Scott was busily engaged in something he appeared to enjoy, Woodward gathered his nerves and put the rest of his plan into operation. He dressed quickly in a protective suit and stepped into the cooling chamber. He stopped in front of the Unisol closest to him, kneeling down in front of the man, as if he were about to propose.

"GR 74, can you hear me?"

GR 74 nodded, sluggish, inert, at rest.

Woodward wet his lips nervously and plunged on. "Sergeant Scott has issued an order. Will you follow that order?"

Order was a magic word to a Unisol. Each and every one of them lived for orders. They thrived on them, welcomed them. GR 74's eyes popped open at the sound of the word, alert. "I will follow my orders."

"Good." Woodward took a grenade from the Unisol's belt, pulled the pin and placed the bomb in GR 74's hand, closing his fingers over the firing mechanism. "Sergeant Scott wants you to hold this for thirty seconds. When thirty seconds have passed you must let go. Do you understand?"

GR 74 nodded. "I understand."

"Start counting backwards from thirty," said Woodward, backing out of the chamber, "from now . . ." He stepped out of the room and quickly stripped off the protective suit.

"Thirty . . . twenty-nine . . . twenty-eight . . ."

Woodward was on his way to the exit; he slipped out the door just as GR 74 hit number twenty-two.

Once outside, he walked around the far side of the truck and disappeared into the night, grateful to be alive.

Scott had beaten two truckers half to death and was now holding a third bruised and bloodied man up by his ankle. Blood streamed out of his nose and flowed to the dirty asphalt.

"Now," said Scott, "will you tell me what I need to know?"

The man choked on his own blood as he tried to speak. "I saw them on the road," the man managed to gasp. "I passed them on the road a couple of hours back."

Andrew Scott lowered the man, slamming his head into the unforgiving pavement, like a pile driver. "Where did they go?"

"They were headed East on I-16."

"Good." Scott dumped the man unceremoniously on the ground. Just as the man hit, the grenade nestled in GR 74's hand exploded. Smoke and flame burst from the Unisol truck. Electronic circuits burned out in a flash, and fire erupted from the seams of the big vehicle. The metal plates bowed outward, but didn't smash—the truck had been built to withstand attacks far more serious than a single grenade.

The truckers in the lot dove for safety. But not Scott. The instant the explosion detonated, he raced for the truck, diving into the maelstrom of smoke and flame, battling his way into the inferno. It was a disaster area. The cooling chamber had split open, and the Unisols not killed instantly by the blast were overheating and splitting open. The regeneration tanks had ruptured, and the fluid was ankle-deep on the command center floor.

But some of the Unisols were still alive. Two of them were on fire, burning brightly. Scott pounced on them, spraying them with a canister of coolant, then stamping out the flames on their clothing with his heavy boots. He seized them by the sleeves and pulled them out the door.

The truckers were still flattened on their stomachs in the parking lot, scarcely daring to raise their heads. When they looked up, they saw a very scary sight—Andrew Scott standing over them, a crazed and wild look in his eyes, holding in each hand the smoking body of an injured Unisol.

Scott slung the two bodies into the cab of the Unisol truck and then climbed up after them, sliding in behind the wheel. He hit the gas and twisted the key. For a few agonized seconds, the engine strained and coughed, and Scott muttered under his breath as he willed the stricken truck into life. He leaned on the controls, as if trying to transfer his own great strength to the motor. Scott pumped the gas all the way to the floor, and suddenly, with a great gout of black smoke, the engine turned over. Scott slammed the vehicle into gear and muscled the truck onto the highway, leaving behind him some very relieved truckers.

Andrew Scott was like a man possessed, consumed by his desire to find and then kill Luc Devreux and his female accomplice. It was all coming back to him, those last tortured moments of his real life, those minutes in the flaming village of Tsao Li. Scott had been betrayed— traitors were everywhere—and the most heinous traitor of them all was not Perry and not Garth; it wasn't even Woodward—although in time he would find the scientist and kill him for his treachery. The greatest traitor of all was Luc Devreux, the man who had killed him all those years ago. Now it was payback time.

But Scott wanted firepower on his side. When he found his foe, he would take care of him personally, but in the meantime he needed assistance, and there were no better soldiers on the planet than the remaining Unisols, assuming he could put them back together again.

Ten or twelve miles down the road from the unlucky truck stop, Scott saw the bright lights of a strip mall, a small roadside shopping center. There was a sign the size of a mainsail at the entrance to the mall, lit up like a Christmas tree, advertising the various merchants within. The Unisol truck went streaking into the lot and screeched to a halt.

Scott hefted the two Unisols out of the truck and, a hand on each collar, dragged them through the electronic doors of the mall. He walked through the avenue of shops—the Gap, Thom McAnn, K-Mart—looking at each sign intently. He knew what he was looking for. The bodies slid along behind, greased on treads of their own blood. The sound system played a tinny rendition of "Up, Up and Away" . . .

Shoppers stopped dead in their tracks as Scott passed, then shrieked and ran. Some just gaped, thinking that this must be some kind of promotional stunt for the Octoplex Theater showing the latest action movie. Some patrons were so intent on shopping that they didn't even notice the gory little procession.

The doors of the giant Y-Pay-Mor supermarket swung open to admit Andrew Scott and his two inert companions. At the checkout lines people saw him and dropped to the floor. Mothers grabbed their children and covered their eyes. There were loud screams of alarm when people caught sight of the Heckler and Koch submachine gun slung over Scott's shoulder. As people ran for cover, they wondered if they were about to become a gruesome story on the evening news—yet another massacre by a disgruntled former employee.

But just as some of the shoppers in the mall concourse hadn't noticed Scott as he passed, so some in the supermarket, caught up in their work, just didn't see him. In the middle of the store, a box boy was bent over his labor, sealing a crate of returns with a staple gun. Scott snatched the stapler out of his hand.

"Hey!" The box boy looked up into the terrifying visage. "Holy shit!"

"I need this," said Scott.

"All yours, man."

"You got a meat locker?"

The kid nodded, never taking his wide eyes from Scott's painted, muddied, bloodied face. "Uh-huh."

"Where?"

The box boy pointed. "Back of the store."

"Thank you." Scott walked by with the two bloodied Unisols, passing the kid like a bad dream.

There was a butcher in the giant meat locker, working among hanging sides of beef as a librarian potters in the stacks. He heard the door open, stepped out from the row of carcasses and looked at his visitor.

"Get out," ordered Scott.

The man didn't need a second invitation. He put down his cleaver and ran.

Scott dumped the two Unisols on the hard cold floor and began emptying boxes of dry ice on their smashed-up bodies. Then he knelt down next to one of them and raised the unconscious man's arm. There was a bad shrapnel wound running from his shoulder all the way down to his elbow, revealing a great slice of the meat of his upper arm. The skin flapped over, a bloody sheet. Without hesitating, Scott folded the flap over the torn seam of skin and brought the staple gun to bear, shooting the metal studs into the arm, stapling his comrade back in shape.

He worked feverishly on both men, meeting success with GR 55 but striking out with GR 34. There was no denying that GR 34 was dead and that there was nothing Scott could do to save him. GR 55, however, was quick to mend. He sat up when he had cooled sufficiently and eagerly took the slabs of beef that Scott handed him. He devoured the raw meat, getting instant strength from the food. In a split second he was in a feeding frenzy, tearing at the bloody meat with his sharp teeth and throwing his head back to wolf it down. Blood streamed down his chin and spattered on his uniform.

Scott stood over GR 34, shaking the dead soldier, trying to force life back into him. He felt the anger building. "Get up, soldier!" he yelled. "That's an order!"

The magic word did nothing for GR 34. He would never respond to another order.

"I said stand to attention, Private! Stand up!"

Frustrated, Scott struck out, kicking at GR 34's corpse. "Turncoat!" The ribs snapped in the dead body. He turned on his heel and grabbed GR 55. Together they walked out of the frigid room and into the relative warmth of the air-conditioned supermarket.

"I am surrounded by insurgent, traitoring fucks!" The two men were marching toward the front of the store, where a group of onlookers gawked at them, protected behind a row of four state troopers.

When Scott saw the people, he stopped and harangued them, trying to win them over to his way of thinking. "Do you have any idea what it's like?" he yelled at the crowd. "Do you? I mean, I'm fighting this thing, man. It's kick ass or kiss ass and I'm bustin' heads. It's the only way to win this fucking war!"

Scott paced in front of the terrified audience. "And these shit heads . . . these yellow traitoring motherfuckers! They're everywhere. You can't trust 'em." He fixed his gaze on a woman in the crowd and shook his head. "Nope, can't trust 'em. No, sir. The only way to teach 'em is to kill 'em." He put his hands on his hips. "And I'm gonna teach 'em all," he said, like a politician making a campaign promise.

If he had expected applause, he was disappointed. Instead, one of the state troopers raised his weapon. "Let's hold it right there, okay, son?"

Andrew Scott seemed surprised to see the troopers. He gawked as if he hadn't realized they had been there all the time. "What?"

"Don't move."

Scott looked to GR 55 as if for sympathy. "They're everywhere," he muttered. Then, as if they were just one body instead of two, the Unisols whipped out their pistols and fired, two shots each. All four bullets slammed home, dropping the four state troopers with four slugs to the forehead. They fell like tenpins.

In the moment that followed the only sound that could be heard was the squawk of static and feedback on a radio clipped to the belt of one of the slain state troopers. Scott knelt and snatched a walkie-talkie from the dead man's belt.

Then, as the reality of what had happened sunk in, the crowd surged and bucked, trying to get away. The screams of the panicked people drowned out Andrew Scott's bitter words.

He kicked at one of the bodies. "Traitors," he spat. "Traitors everywhere."

Chapter Eleven

Luc lay semi-conscious in a bathtub just off the study of Dr. Christopher Gregor. Ice covered him up to the chin, and his head lolled back in the tub, his mind drifting from stupor to lucidity. He could hear voices, quiet and subdued, in the room beyond, and through the open door he could make out the hazy outline of the man and woman, Gregor and Veronica. From time to time Veronica came into the bathroom to check on him, moving the ice over him, the way a mother might rearrange the blankets on a sleeping child.

Veronica and the doctor sat facing each other in the deep leather armchairs in his study. They leaned forward in their chairs, speaking softly, as if exchanging confidences.

"Luc was twenty-five," said Dr. Gregor soberly, "when he was killed in Vietnam."

At first she wasn't quite sure she had heard

correctly. "He was killed in Vietnam? You mean he really *was* dead?"

Gregor nodded. "He was killed in June of 1969. His entire platoon was wiped out."

"Unbelievable! You mean to tell me he's been dead since June of 1969?"

"Well, not dead exactly. They kept him frozen cryogenically for over twenty years. They did it to all the subjects in the experiment."

"Wait a minute . . . Twenty-five in 1969?" Veronica did some fast mental arithmetic. "That makes him . . . That makes him fifty years old!"

Dr. Gregor smiled grimly. "You could say that. Or you could say he's four years old. That's when we brought him back to life."

Veronica was a mass of raw emotion. Suddenly, she realized that she had feeling for Luc she hadn't *known* she had until that very moment. She was glad he was alive, sickened that he had died once and simply bewildered at the notion of his being brought back to life. She was sure of one thing, though—he was whole and human and had feelings too, inchoate, nascent feelings, but they were undeniably emotions that came from the heart of a man.

She tried to gather her thoughts, her brain still reeling at the doctor's eerie words, spoken so naturally. "Brought back to life . . . I don't— How? Who did this?"

"You see, Stafford Industries wanted to make the perfect soldiers. Fighting machines that would be strong, genetically engineered and reinforced. But without souls."

"Without souls! I can't believe this! It's too horrific!"

Dr. Gregor tried reasoning with her. "You have to see it from their point of view. The originators of this project saw it as a way of saving lives. No man would ever die in the service of his country. They could just, well, recycle, as it were."

Veronica wasn't buying it. Her natural skepticism kicked into action. "Oh yeah, that Stafford Industries has a heart of gold. Die in the service of your country? Or die in the service of the highest bidder?" Stafford was a sprawling conglomerate well known for its hundreds of millions of profit in arms sales, everything from simple handguns to complicated weapons systems. "Each one of these . . . these things would be built by Stafford, right? They would hold the patent and if the program worked they could sell these soldiers to every third-world crazy going wild high-teching his army."

Gregor nodded sadly. "I guess that would have been a possibility."

"How could you have been part of this?" she demanded.

The doctor shook his head. "I've been asking myself that question for years. I suppose I was seduced . . . seduced by the unlimited money for research, the chance to break ground in my field." He passed a hand through his white hair. "But that doesn't excuse it, does it?"

"No," she said shortly. "It doesn't." The truth was awful, the tale the doctor told grotesque, but it was, she had to admit, an even better story than she had hoped for. The reporter in her shifted to high gear. Veronica tried to compose herself, to banish her disordered feelings and concentrate on the details of the biggest story of her career.

"Okay, doctor, how did it work?"

"It's rather complicated."

"I'm no scientist, Doctor, and I don't know a thing about genetics. Try explaining it in layman's language."

"Well . . ." Christopher Gregor groped for words. "You see, by hyperaccelerating the body we discovered that we could make dead tissue live again. But to make the process work, the bodies ran at dangerously high temperatures and needed to be cooled constantly." He nodded toward the bathroom door and Luc submerged in his icy bath. "Their brain waves needed to be kept under control, sedated and controlled, or they would eventually get hit by a cranial seizure, a massive stroke."

Veronica Roberts shook her head quickly. "I don't get it. Just what are you saying?"

"I'm saying that the process is only partially successful. You've seen how the subjects operate in the short term. Over a matter of hours they perform beautifully . . ."

"But?"

"But they also have to be baby-sat constantly,

fine-tuned every six to eight hours. They couldn't exist without the substantial backup they have."

Veronica thought of the giant Universal Soldier command truck, and although she hadn't seen much of it, she remembered that the interior was crammed with equipment. "And without the support system?"

Gregor breathed deeply. "The soldiers aren't really alive, not in the sense that we are . . ."

Veronica pointed through the bathroom door. "He's alive!" she insisted.

"Yes and no . . . I'm saying that without his treatments Luc's body and mind will degenerate back into normal human tissue."

"That's good, right? How could that not be good?"

"Well," said Dr. Gregor, "we aren't exactly sure what will happen. Theoretically, he could turn into the person he once was. He certainly wouldn't have the powers he has now, and in a matter of months he would become his biological age. He wouldn't look fifty, he probably wouldn't even *feel* fifty. But there would be that kind of wear and tear on his vital organs. Of course, in order for him to revert to his normal state he would have to be under the care of one of the team physicians. He would have to be led back to his former self. What has been done to him would have to be undone, to a certain degree."

"So he could still die?" asked Veronica.

"Yes," said Dr. Gregor shortly. "Any patient

who has undergone serious surgery would die without a doctor's care."

"I'm shocked . . . I can't begin to fathom what's going on here . . ."

The maid knocked softly at the door and walked in. She was trembling, frightened. "Dr. Gregor?"

"What is it, Maria?"

She glanced nervously at Veronica. "On the television, Doctor."

Dr. Gregor picked up the TV remote control and clicked on the set, turning to an all-news cable channel.

Veronica recognized the face, but didn't know the man's name. "That's the guy from the truck."

The screen was filled with a still picture of Colonel Perry, and the voice-over from the announcer was suitably somber.

". . . killed early this morning. Authorities are still seeking the whereabouts of Veronica Roberts . . ." Perry's photograph was replaced with an old press-pass picture of Veronica. She gasped when she saw her own image on the screen.

". . . the CNA reporter believed to be linked to the two deaths."

"Two deaths?" said Gregor.

The very thought of Huey's death was painful. "My cameraman. He got killed . . ." She couldn't quite remember when it was. "Last night? The night before? It all seems like it was so long ago."

The story on the television news had changed.

"And a bizarre incident in Arizona turned deadly . . ."

"They've set you up," said the doctor.

But Veronica wasn't paying attention. Her eyes were locked on the screen. "Oh my God . . ."

"The incident was captured by the supermarket security cameras," intoned the anchorwoman.

Andrew Scott's murderous face appeared, his wild eyes glinting in the sharp, harsh light of the supermarket.

"That's him! That's the one who killed Huey!" Veronica shouted.

Scott was glaring at the camera. ". . . It's kick ass or kiss ass and I'm bustin' heads. It's the only way to win this (bleep) war!"

Dr. Gregor snapped off the television set, worried but perfectly aware of what was going on. "Regressive traumatic recall," he said, as if making a mental note.

"What's that?"

"Trauma inflicted at the moment of his death. For Luc, that manifested itself in his desire to go home. When he awoke as a Unisol, he returned to that single emotion. For Scott . . ." Gregor shrugged his shoulders. "He thinks he's still in Vietnam fighting a war that ended two decades ago. He doesn't realize he's alive."

"He's not."

Veronica and Gregor looked to the doorway. Luc was standing there, dressed and looking grave. "He's dead. Just like me."

There was an awkward silence. They had not

realized that he was listening. The stillness of the room was broken only by the far-off whine of police sirens. Gregor walked to the window and glanced out. Police cruisers were streaking across the hospital grounds, converging on his neat little house.

Veronica was on her feet. She didn't have to be told that the police were coming for her and Luc. "How the hell did they find us?"

The maid answered nervously. "I'm sorry," she said, trembling on the verge of tears. "I called them. When I saw your picture on the television . . ."

The doctor moved to comfort her. "It's all right, Maria. You didn't know . . ."

Luc's mind was kicking into high gear. "Do you have a car?"

Gregor tossed him the keys to his car. "It's behind the house. Take the street to the gate. You might be able to get out by the rear gate."

Gregor's worries for Luc's physical state were foremost in Veronica's mind. "Are you sure you know what you're doing? You can't go on like this."

The sirens were growing louder. It was only a matter of seconds before the police came busting through the door.

But there was only one thing on Luc's mind. "I'm going home," he said.

Chapter Twelve

Dr. Gregor's car, a big, powerful Lincoln with all the options, zoomed across the hospital grounds, clearing the exit of the complex before the first patrolman rapped on the front door of the doctor's house.

Luc drove fast, heading for downtown Clinton, hardly braking at red lights and streaking through stop signs. The hospital was on the outskirts of the little town, and the fast car chewed up the few miles in a matter of minutes. The center of Clinton wasn't much—just a single, old-fashioned main street, lined with a few shops, storefront offices and, at the far end, the town's small bus station, the depot that connected Clinton to the rest of the world.

The Lincoln came to a screeching halt in front of the bus station, and Luc muscled the car into a parking spot.

"Why are you stopping?" Veronica looked

around worriedly, as if expecting to see the police converging on them. But the sleepy street and tiny bus depot were placid. Some elderly women were window shopping in front of the Wal-Mart, a couple of Trailways buses were drawn up in the forecourt of the bus station, waiting for their departure time to roll around. It was the quiet, sort of dull scene that one might find anywhere in small town America.

The one thing she failed to note was the man sitting in one of the seats of the two-chair barber shop across from the bus station, his face wreathed in hot towels. The barber was standing over him, giving him a nice clean crew cut. It was the haircutter's habit to keep an eye on the street as he worked, and he couldn't fail to notice the big car driven by a man in a tattered army uniform.

"Say, Sheriff," said the barber, "think you ought to take a look at this . . ."

"Take a look at what?" The reply was muffled slightly by the steaming towels.

The barber stripped off the hot cloths and pointed through his dusty window. "That . . ."

The sheriff heaved himself out of the commodious chair and watched through narrowed eyes as Luc walked into the bus station. Then he grabbed the phone in the shop and started dialing quickly . . .

Luc was only in the depot for a minute or two. He emerged carrying a handful of road maps and spread them on the hood of the car, staring intently, plotting his course out of Clinton.

Veronica tugged at his uniform sleeve, trying to pull him back into the car.

"This is crazy," she insisted. "You heard what the doctor said, right? You need medical help. You have to turn yourself in, start the treatments again. It's the only way . . ."

Slowly, Luc tore his eyes from the map. He looked at her for a moment before answering, as if really pondering her words. "I turn myself in . . . And then?"

"Then we'll expose everything. Dr. Gregor will help us. We'll *get* those bastards. The ones who did this to you, to Huey . . ."

Wearily, Luc shook his head. "Look, I don't want a parade and I don't want to be a hero. The pieces of my life are starting to come back together again. I have to get back home."

For an instant, Veronica wished that he had died with a desire for revenge, rather than this fervent need to get home. "If you don't go back to Gregor, you'll die!"

"I'm already dead," said Luc quietly.

"No you're not!" she shouted. "You're alive, goddammit! That's a precious thing!"

"You know nothing about it," he said.

Now Veronica was angry. She grabbed him by the lapels and held him in front of her, her eyes blazing. "The hell I don't! I've been through this before . . . I was married. Three years ago I watched my husband die of cancer." Her voice softened, her angry words tempered by the old grief. "Watching him wither away was the most painful experience of my life. I don't think I could *ever* go through that again."

"I'm sorry," said Luc soberly. "I did not know."

Veronica shrugged as if shaking off a mantle of old sorrow. "What happened then isn't important now. I'm just telling you this because I'm not going to stand by and watch you do this to yourself."

Luc had already considered that possibility. He took a bus ticket from his pocket and handed it to her. She looked at it as if she had never seen one before.

"What is this? What do you think you're doing?"

"It is a ticket to Los Angeles. You must leave here quickly. It is not safe."

"What! I know it's not safe. It hasn't been safe for days. You think I'm going to leave *now*?"

"It is not safe as long as you're with me. He's only after me now. You have your story. Isn't that what you wanted?"

Veronica felt the hurt flare in her. This whole thing had become much more than a story to her, and she was saddened to think that was all he made of it. "You're wrong . . . And you're making a big mistake."

Luc nodded, accepting her words, but his mind was made up. The hydraulic doors of the bus behind them hissed open. "That is your bus," he said.

Veronica gazed at him for a moment, trying to

think of words that would make sense to him, trying to convey to him the depth of the feelings she had for him. As if sensing what she was about to say, Luc turned away.

Veronica's face fell, disappointed that she seemed to mean nothing to him. She walked toward the bus, her head down.

Luc returned to the Lincoln, the maps still spread on the wide hood. He heard the doors of the bus whoosh closed, and in spite of himself, he looked up to see her leave, hoping he could catch a last glimpse of her. Luc scanned the dark windows but could not see her. He returned to the map, trying to trace a direct route across Texas in the direction of Louisiana, but aware of a gnawing, a human longing for the woman he had just lost.

He looked up again as the big bus pulled out of the lot. The vehicle lumbered by, revealing another bus, and standing in front of it, like a little girl lost, was Veronica. She smiled sheepishly and shrugged.

He smiled back and then took a step toward her. Just as he reached her, the next bus fired up and moved off, sweeping aside like a curtain in front of a stage, exposing a wall of police cars, at least twenty-five. Each had both front doors open, and resting on them were cops, their guns aimed squarely at Luc and Veronica. Her head whipped around. Everywhere she looked she saw cops and guns.

"Uh-oh," she said.

The sheriff stepped out in front of his men, like a conductor directing an orchestra. "Hold it right there, you two. Come quietly and there won't be any trouble . . ."

Veronica looked worriedly to Luc. She could see his eyes darting here and there to all sides, his mind working. He was trained to avoid capture, to always stay on the attack—he had to make some kind of move. It was bred into him.

Veronica knew suicide when she saw it. She clutched at his sleeve. "Don't do it . . ."

The sheriff, assisted by a couple of deputies, placed them under arrest, snapping on the cuffs and reading them their rights. Veronica swung into her act, attempting to bluster her way to freedom—she knew that it was largely pointless, but she would have hated herself if she hadn't at least tried.

"I have important information that must be delivered to the Army immediately," she said urgently. "Information that must be delivered by me and my companion personally. I know I can speak for the government, Sheriff, when I say that any assistance you can render will be gratefully acknowledged and rewarded by the authorities, who—"

The sheriff laughed. "Okay, little lady, why don't you just can the bullshit? You'll get your day in court." He waved over to some of the cops, and immediately another bus, a machine that looked like a fortified school bus, burst into life and rolled over to them. Stenciled on the side were the words "Ashton County Police Prisoner Transport."

The back door swung open, and Luc and Veronica were loaded into the vehicle, their handcuffs chained to rings on the steel sides of the compartment.

"Hey, Bob!" The sheriff shouted to a man hovering at the edge of the scene. "Get the hell over here!"

Bob came rushing over, raising a camera and snapping off a couple of pictures of the sheriff. Then he focused on Luc and Veronica chained in their mobile prison.

"You all don't mind a little picture do you?"

Veronica did her best to shrug, but it wasn't easy with her hands tethered.

"Got an election comin' up," the sheriff explained as Luke snapped away.

"Good luck," said Veronica.

"Thank you, miss. Okay, Bob. That's enough." The sheriff shooed away the photographer and then started to swing the steel door shut.

"Sheriff," Veronica pleaded. "Do you by any chance have a cigarette?"

"Sorry," he said with a smile. "I quit." He slammed the door and locked it.

It was pretty fair to say that Clinton, New Mexico, was not exactly a hotbed of serious crime. Beyond the occasional bar fight, some drunk driving and a domestic dispute or two, there wasn't a whole hell of a lot of excitement for the law officers in the town, so the cops that were standing around the prisoner transport bus were indulging in a little self-congratulation. They had nailed the two bad drug dealer—murderers that had eluded the feds and the Army in two other states.

One cop slapped Sheriff Dempsey on the back. "Way to go, Nathan. Bagged a big one this time."

Sheriff Dempsey's chest swelled with pride. "Well, they just picked the wrong town, that's all," doing his best to sound aw-shucks modest.

Another policeman, standing a few yards off, was jabbering into a walkie-talkie, busily telling his wife of the heroics on Main Street. "That's right, Sharon," he said excitedly, "Nathan picked them up at the bus depot and they're taking them to County lockup over in Ashton . . ."

But Sharon wasn't the only one listening in on the cop's breathless retelling of the story. His voice came loud and clear into the cab of the Unisol command truck. GR 55 was at the wheel of the massive vehicle, and Scott was in the passenger seat, the radio receiver between them.

"They're taking I-18 out of town," said the police officer. "They should get there just after lunch . . ."

When Scott heard the route, he smiled triumphantly at his companion. "Now we have them," he said.

GR 55 nodded and pressed down hard on the accelerator, the big truck leaping forward on the road.

• • •

The little convoy made its way along the interstate, rumbling toward the small county seat of Ashton. One police cruiser led the file, followed by the prisoner transport bus and then a second police car bringing up the rear. No one really expected any trouble, so there were only three cops detailed to protect the prisoner bus, one in the lead car, two in the rear.

Inside the bus, Luc was edgy and uncomfortable, nervous at being restrained. He had been trained to resist capture and, if taken, to get free at any cost. He tested his chains, leaning his weight into them, and he could tell that if need be, he could break free. But once he did that, where would he go? There were two glass windows in the rear door of the bus, but they were far too small for either of them to wriggle through. There was a heavy, armored trapdoor connecting the prisoner area with the cab. Maybe he could break through that, but there was no way he could do it without alerting the driver.

Even more worrisome was the plight of Veronica. The moment he launched his escape attempt, things would get hot. Luc didn't much care what happened to him, but how would he see her through the breakout without her getting hurt?

"Why didn't you leave when you had the chance?"

"What? And miss all the fun?"

Luc's sense of humor hadn't developed quite as

well as the rest of him. He looked unconvinced by her flippancy.

"Okay. Maybe you *are* more than just a story to me . . . Look," she said, suddenly serious, "maybe this is the best thing that could have happened. The cops may have gotten us, but at least they aren't going to *kill* us. This is a chance to clear up this mess. It's kind of like protective custody . . ."

"It's not the police I'm worried about," said Luc soberly. He tensed suddenly, cocking his head, listening intently. Beneath the rumbling of the bus engine and the rushing of the desert wind he could hear something, a terrible sound.

"What?" she said. "What?"

It was a sound he had known almost all his life as a Universal Soldier. It was the unmistakable, growling, rumbling note of the Unisol command truck.

"He's found us," said Luc.

There was quite a concentration of military installations in the Southwest, so the giant army truck growing ever bigger in the rearview mirror of the trailing police car was not a strange sight to the two cops.

The truck bore down on the cruiser, zooming up at a great rate of speed and then slowing down, sitting on the tail of the car, looming big and brawny, filling the rear window. A blast like an artillery barrage sounded from the truck's huge air horns.

The cop behind the wheel stuck his hand out the window and waved the Unisol truck past, but the vehicle remained where it was, right on top of the cruiser's bumper.

"Goddam Army thinks it owns the road," the driver grumbled. He waved vigorously. "Go ahead! Pass, for crying out loud."

GR 55 guided the truck out into the passing lane, standing alongside the cop car, towering above it like a super-tanker over a rowboat.

It was obvious that the army vehicle had more than enough power to pass the escort car and the bus in a matter of seconds, but it lingered, unnerving the two policemen.

"What the hell are you playing at?" yelled the cop behind the wheel.

As if in answer, the Unisol truck swerved into the police cruiser, slamming into it, slapping it off the road as if it weighed no more than a bicycle. The car sailed up and over the embankment next to the road, turning in midair, flipping over and crashing flat on its roof.

The driver of the bus, a highway patrolman, heard the crash and immediately grabbed his microphone. "Jesus Christ! What the hell was that? Jackson? Do you copy? Jackson?"

Luc and Veronica heard the crash. He tore at the chains on the steel walls, pulling them free from the brackets. He snapped the handcuffs in two, freeing himself. He fell on Veronica's restraints, making short work of them.

She rubbed her wrists and tried to mask her

fear with a feeble joke. "Never a cop around when you need one, huh?"

Luc was peering out of the rear window. He caught a glimpse of the Unisol truck and Andrew Scott leaning out of the passenger side of the cab, the Heckler and Koch submachine gun in his hands. Luc dove for cover, and a split second later both windows blew out, the wasplike bullets howling in the enclosed steel space.

Luc fell on Veronica, pulling her to the floor, shielding her body with his. Sharp shards of glass showered.

The cop in the lead car, all alone, was spooked by the sound of gunfire. Instead of heroics, he got on his microphone.

"Holy shit!" he screeched. "Send reinforcements!"

Scott had the truck pull up next to the bus, and he peppered the transport with bullets. "Where are you going, Devreux!" he screamed between bursts. "You cannot escape from me!"

The driver of the bus was trying to do three things simultaneously. First, he was fighting to keep the vehicle on the road. Second, he was attempting to keep the vehicle on the road but without actually watching the road—he wanted to keep his head down below dashboard level. Third, he was struggling to get his gun out of the holster under his arm.

The Unisol truck was pulling level with the cab, Scott leaning out of the window, smiling derisively at the terrified driver. "Looking for something?" he asked. "Too late."

The driver sat up and gaped at Scott as he opened fire. Flame shot from the barrel, the bullets slamming into the driver's head and neck, shredding him. Blood and flesh splattered onto the windshield, and in an instant the highway patrolman was dead. He slipped down under the steering wheel, falling heavily onto the accelerator.

The bus was out of control now, fishtailing off the highway and onto the rough terrain next to the road. GR 55 downshifted and lifted the Unisol truck off the ribbon of road, thundering across the desert in hot pursuit.

Scott was screaming out the window. "Did you really think you could run away back to your farm in Louisiana?" Another rip of bullets stitched across the bus. "You can't desert me!"

Both Luc and Veronica were lying flat on the floor, wincing as the bullets whipped around the room.

"What do we do now?" she managed to gasp.

"We must stop the bus."

She rolled her eyes. "Gee, why didn't I think of that?"

The bus crashed into a thicket of small trees and undergrowth and plowed through, bouncing over the uneven ground. The Unisol truck slowed down and tucked in behind the bus, following in its path, slipstreaming through the vegetation.

Luc got to his feet and charged at the armored

door, punching his full weight into the metal panel, but on the first rush it held firm. He braced himself against the walls and kicked at the door, pounding it with his heavy boots.

The bus rocketed through the copse and out onto the flat, hard-packed surface of a dry lake bed, a shallow brown basin set in the desert floor.

The Unisol truck zoomed up alongside the prisoner transport. Scott was hanging perilously far out of the cab, a hand grenade in his hand.

"Devreux!" he yelled into the wind. "Devreux, catch! You'll get a bang out of this!" He pulled the pin in the bomb and lobbed it through the shattered rear window.

Veronica paled when she saw it. She fell on the grenade, grabbing it before it slid under the benches that lined both sides of the holding area.

"What the hell do I do with this?"

Luc turned away from the door, his eyes widening when he saw what she held in her hand. "Get rid of it!"

Veronica tossed the bomb out of the rear window. It detonated a second later, gouging a crater in the dry lake bed.

Luc was working hard on the door, slamming the lock. The door was dented and the catch was beginning to give.

Scott laughed when he saw the effect of his first grenade. He was enjoying himself. "So, you want to play catch?"

The next grenade came sailing through the rear window, and Veronica scrambled to get it. She grabbed the lethal dose of explosive and tossed it, aiming it this time. She missed her target— Scott's open window—but she was close enough to the mark. The grenade sailed over the cab, detonating a few inches above the metal roof. Shrapnel clattered against the armor, but the concussion of the blast rocked the truck. Scott recovered quickly from the explosion.

The third grenade came through the window. "Now, isn't this fun?" Scott called after it.

The grenade bounced on the steel floor and skittered by Veronica, rolling under the bench. Instantly, she was on her knees, feeling in the shadows for the bomb.

"Oh please, oh please, oh please . . ." she whimpered. Her hand almost closed over the grenade, but in that instant the bus bumped and the bomb rolled away from her slippery palms.

Luc charged the door and finally tore it off the hinges. "Get over here!" he yelled to Veronica, grabbing her by the scruff of her neck.

"I can't find it!" she shouted desperately.

The grenade bounced from under the bench and bumped toward the back of the bus, ricocheting off the door. Luc hauled her into the driver's cab just as it detonated. The cramped space filled with smoke and the noise was deafening, the force of the explosion throwing Luc and Veronica to the floor.

The burning bus and the Unisol truck thundered out of the lake bed, making straight for the few shacks of a hardscrabble farm that had flourished back in the days when there was water in the lake. Now it was just scraping by with a few chickens.

The farmer jerked awake on the porch of his tumbledown house when he heard a grenade going off. His mouth dropped open as the two huge vehicles, side by side, rushed toward the flimsy buildings. The bus smashed into the barn, thundered across the hay-strewn floor and blasted through the far side in a cloud of straw and chicken feathers.

The Unisol truck bashed through the farmhouse, tearing the building to pieces, emerging with a tangle of household articles caught on its antennae and wrapped around its wheels. In a matter of seconds the whole farm had been reduced to a blown-away ruin.

The farmer stared after the racing vehicles. "Hey!" he said.

Luc was struggling with the corpse of the driver tangled in the wheel of the bus, desperate to get the bus under control before it careened off the road. He shot a quick glance out of the window and saw that he had to get command of the wheel immediately. The road they were on was headed directly for a cliff, a drop from the top of the mesa into the canyon below. He had to pull the bus into a sharp right-hand turn or go over the edge.

Luc threw all his strength behind the wheel, turning it hand over hand, yanking the bus into the turn with a scream of tires and smoking rubber.

The bus teetered on the edge of the drop, two wheels tilting up off the asphalt. For a long, terrible second it seemed as if the bus would throw itself over the side; then it appeared to change its mind and heaved over like a sailboat falling off the wind. The Unisol truck was right behind it, power-sliding into the turn, Scott screaming with laughter like a maniac.

Luc could see to the end of the road. It curved in a semicircle and finished in a dead end, right before the edge of another dangerous precipice. It was nothing more than a panoramic lookout placed there for the benefit of tourists who bothered to make the long drive off the interstate for a beautiful view of deep desert canyons.

Luc had given up trying to control the bus. The speed and the frozen controls made it virtually impossible. Veronica saw that they were racing toward certain death. "What do we do now?"

"We jump," said Luc.

"Why did I ask?"

He slammed open the door and wrapped his arms around Veronica, hoping to cushion what promised to be a hard fall.

"Jump!"

Veronica sailed into the void, but out of Luc's protecting arms. Just as he was supposed to go, his sleeve snagged on a hinge, pulling him back into the bus cab.

Scott watched the girl go and whooped triumphantly. If she survived the fall, he would come back and finish her off later. *Now* he had Devreux trapped. He lofted another grenade, judging the distance, drawing a bead on the underside of the bus.

The bomb exploded beneath the undercarriage, the force of the blast directed directly upward, smashing into the bottom of the bus, picking the whole vehicle up and throwing it on its side.

With a terrible rasping of tortured metal, the bus slid toward the edge. With only a few yards to go, it slithered to a stop, just a few feet from the lip of the precipice.

The Unisol truck was blundering toward the inert bus, like a charging bull.

"You're going over, Farm Boy!"

Luc threw his upper body through the driver's side window, the dead cop's pistol in his hand. Hardly pausing to steady himself, he blasted all six shots in the magazine straight through the cab of the Unisol truck. The six bullets found their mark, smashing into GR 55's face, blowing away his cheek and jaw, driving deeply into his brain. His shattered skull fell forward on the wheel, and his leaden foot pressed hard on the accelerator.

Luc struggled out of the bus and ran its length, ready to jump.

Scott was oblivious to the danger. He screamed in wild triumph. "Got you, Farm Boy!"

Chapter Thirteen

The vehicles went over the side with a rumbling like thunder. The Unisol truck, crammed with ammunition and grenades, blasted and blew with a dozen secondary explosions. The two vehicles, locked together, two fused, hot lumps of metal, fell end over end, smashing on the rocky floor of the canyon.

Veronica had stumbled to her feet and staggered to the edge of the cliff. She peered over, scared of what she would see. The truck and the bus were a mass of flame and smoke, black and orange, the fire brighter than the sun, the smoke as dark as the night. A hollow column of dust rose off the sides of the precipice, marking the vehicles' rocky fall to the bottom of the ravine.

"Luc!" she screamed. Her voice came back to her, an anguished echo, rocketing off the stone walls of the canyon.

"Over here . . ." A few yards away, caught in a

small formation of boulders, lay Luc. He was broken and bloodied, his uniform tunic in tatters.

A wave of relief broke over her, and she rushed to him, throwing her arms around him and holding him tight. "Oh, thank God," she said, tears springing into her eyes.

"We have to get out of here . . . ," he said weakly. "We have to keep moving."

Veronica looked down to the canyon floor. The vehicles continued to burn brightly. "I don't think we have to worry about him anymore."

"Come on." He leaned on her shoulder, and together they climbed up the rocky slope of the ravine. They clambered over the edge and found themselves looking straight into the business end of a twelve-gauge shotgun. A cop.

"Okay," he said. "Hold it right there, asshole." His car was parked across the dusty highway, a roadblock of one.

"Nice and easy," he said gruffly, the barrel swinging back and forth as he kept an eye on both of them. "Don't give me a reason."

They were both worn out, too tired to resist. Slowly, Veronica and Luc raised their weary arms above their heads. "That's good," said the cop. "All right, turn around. Get on your hands and knees and put your hands behind your back."

Luc and Veronica followed his instructions to the letter, dropping to their knees in the warm dust. The cop advanced warily, the shotgun aimed at the back of Luc's neck, as if the cop thought that Luc was a wounded bear, downed but still dangerous.

He had a pair of handcuffs out, and as he leaned over to bind Luc's wrists, he took his eyes off Veronica, concentrating on the man, the greater—he thought—threat.

The cop was wrong. As soon as he was occupied with his male prisoner, Veronica leaped to her feet and smashed the cop with both fists on the back of the neck. Fireworks seemed to explode behind his eyes. She pushed aside the weapon and brought her knee straight up into the police officer's crotch. The man doubled over in pain and fell face-first into the dirt.

Luc stared at her, open-mouthed, amazed that she could handle a cop so easily.

"Well, okay. I had three brothers," she explained. "You learn where a guy's weak points are."

"So I see . . ."

Veronica nestled under Luc's shoulder, taking his weight on her small frame. They stumbled toward the car.

She got behind the wheel of the police cruiser and started the engine, gunned it twice and smiled over at her companion.

"Now where?" asked Luc.

"Simple. I'm taking you home." She slid the car into gear and hit the gas hard. "Buckle up," she said.

It was a long way to Louisiana, and they drove hard, stopping only when they had to. By sunset they had crossed into Texas, stopping long enough for Luc to down an enormous amount of junk food and for Veronica to drink enough coffee to stay alert during a long night ride.

By midnight, though, they realized that the air conditioning in the car was not up to the task of keeping Luc cool. They stopped for a few hours at a motel in Abilene, where Luc settled in the bathtub and Veronica cleaned out the ice machine, packing him down till he was cool enough to move on.

They drove through Fort Worth and Dallas just before dawn and were at Shreveport in time for Luc to consume ten or twelve plates of ham and eggs for breakfast. They put gas in the car—along with six bags of ice—and rolled deep into Cajun country.

By the evening of that day they were on the outskirts of Luc's hometown, driving quietly through the deserted streets. Veronica was at the wheel now, and Luc stared out the window at the small town scenes. From time to time, Veronica shot a glance at her companion. His face registered some recognition. He narrowed his eyes, concentrating, as they passed the high school. She could see that he was trying to place the brown brick building and picture himself there—a football player, an honor student, a troublemaker: some role he had played in his distant innocence.

"How you doing?" she asked.

He shook his head. "I remember . . . a lot, but it's not clear. It's like looking through smoke or fog. I don't know . . ." He turned back to the window. "Some things are new," he admitted as they passed a Hyundai dealer's showroom on the main street.

Gradually, they worked their way through town

and out into the countryside again. Luc's face brightened as he recognized more and more. He pointed out a creek he used to swim and fish in, a single-lane blacktop road where he used to ride his bike.

Finally, they turned onto a dirt road. Veronica could feel him tense as the yards passed. They worked their way down the track, rutted as it was with deep grooves that accommodated the wide, heavy tires of tractors and other pieces of agricultural machinery. They were passing under a long arch of cypresses hung with Spanish moss when they caught sight of the farmhouse.

It was just as he had seen in his waking dreams. The house was older than he remembered and it had sagged a little, as if it had fallen on hard times. But the porch was there, with the same wooden furniture, the rocker, the porch swing.

Veronica parked the car, pulling it alongside the battered family Ford station wagon, and killed the lights. There were pieces of farm equipment scattered around the front yard—a couple of rusting plows; a vicious-looking harrow, the steel barrel a mass of spikes. There were two tractors parked near a ramshackle barn and next to that a pickup truck.

They sat for a moment looking at their surroundings, at the machinery and up at the house. No light showed from the curtained windows.

"Maybe there's no one here," she said.

Luc smiled. "Farmers go to bed early."

"Oh. Yeah. Of course." She touched his arm.

217

"Let's go knock on the door. I'm sure they won't mind waking up. Not for this."

She helped him walk to the porch steps and up to the front door. He hesitated for a moment then knocked, softly at first and, when there was no answer, harder, more urgently.

The house remained as still as a crypt. The only sound was the rustle of wind in the trees and, far off, on the horizon the low rumble of thunder as a summer storm blew in from the Gulf.

Luc and Veronica exchanged looks.

"Where can they be?" she asked.

Luc shook his head. "I don't know." He put his hand out to open the door—he knew it would be unlocked, it always was—then stopped.

"I want you to wait in the car," he said.

"The hell I will. I didn't come this far to—"

"They're old," said Luc quietly. "They think I'm *dead*. If they are here, I think I better see them by myself rather than to go barging in with a stranger. I'm sorry . . . it makes sense this way."

Veronica nodded. "I didn't think of that." She turned and walked down the steps of the porch. "Be careful," she said.

Luc nodded and turned the knob, the door creaking open. He walked down the darkened hallway, guiding himself on instinct and memory. It all came back to him in an overwhelming rush—the smells and feel of his youth spent in this old farmhouse. For a moment he was lost in the recollections of the long dead past, the remembrance of happier, more simple days.

Luc reached the living room and dared to snap on the light. The room was just as he remembered it. A worn old sofa, his mother's knitting in a ball resting on the arm, the big armchair next to the fireplace where his father sat every night of his life reading a newspaper and smoking an ancient briarwood pipe.

Standing on a shelf of the bookcase in the corner of the living room was a small gallery of family pictures. Luc and his parents at a state fair smiling into the camera. He must have been ten or twelve years old, his hair sticking up in an unruly cowlick. There were pictures of long forgotten July Fourths and Christmases, grade school outings, 4-H club pageants and Little League games.

The photographs were arranged chronologically, a pictorial history of Luc's short youth. There were a couple of school pictures—tenth grade, eleventh grade—and a more formal portrait, a black and white picture of Luc in his gown and mortarboard. High school graduation. He picked up the picture and stared at it closely. He recognized his youthful features, but couldn't actually believe that it was a picture of him.

Luc replaced the picture, then moved on to the next. It was a photo of him in uniform, the picture the army took for the folks back home when the recruit finished basic. He held it close to his face as if looking for a clue to his own indentity, but it was like looking at another person, a stranger he had never met.

As he replaced the picture on the bookcase

shelf, there was a flash of lightning and a rumble of thunder from the storm that was rolling in.

Then the lights went out.

For a second, Luc stood absolutely still in the darkness, listening to the thunder die, unsure of what had happened. His soldier instincts told him that the lights had gone out because he was about to be under attack; but as Luc Devreux, the man who had grown up in this house, he knew that the electrical supply in that part of Louisiana was subject to interruption; it had never taken much of a storm to bring the lines down. Maybe some things hadn't changed in twenty-five years . . .

He crept into the kitchen. In a flash of lightning he saw enough to know that all was not well. The table had been turned over and broken plates and cups were crunched under his boots. There had been a struggle in that room, a violent fight.

All of Luc's internal alarms triggered. The evil, the danger had followed him into this quiet corner of Louisiana. Now he had to find it and kill it.

Veronica waited by the car, watching the house. She saw the light go on in the living room and nodded to herself. Maybe Luc's parents were there after all. She waited impatiently to be summoned into the house, but when the first drops of rain began to fall, she decided to wait out the storm in the car. But before she could open the door, a hand came out of the wet darkness and closed over her mouth.

Andrew Scott hissed in her ear. "Guess who?"

Chapter Fourteen

Scott was in command, Veronica could tell that in an instant. He dragged her across the muddy lawn in front of the farmhouse past the pickup and the tractor and the pieces of rusting farm equipment half sunk in the wet muck. Scott shoved her into the barn and bound her arms behind her back and gagged her with a strip of burlap torn from an old sack.

It was dark in the barn but there was enough light for her to see that she was not Scott's only captive. In the corner of a stall were two elderly people, a man and a woman, both of them tied up and gagged as she was. They were Luc's parents and Mrs. Devreux looked at her with pleading, uncomprehending eyes.

Scott pushed her to the dusty floor. "Kneel, bitch," he ordered. He walked to the door of the barn and cupped his hands around his mouth.

"Devreux! Nice farm," he yelled. "It's exactly like you described it back in 'Nam."

Inside the farmhouse, Luc froze. Scott! How had he found them?

"Devreux! Do you hear me? Why don't you come out and join our little family reunion?"

Luc's blood ran cold. *Family reunion*. That could only mean that Scott had his parents and Veronica captive. Luc crossed to the hall closet and opened it. It was packed with the odds and ends that families accumulate, but deep in the back behind the raincoats and the rubber boots he found a shotgun, right where his father had always kept it. A box of shells rested on the shelf. He broke the gun and slipped two rounds into the chamber. Then he headed for the front door. It was time to confront Scott once and for all.

Scott's voice broke through the storm. "What are you waiting for, Private? We have some unfinished business, you and me. Do you hear me?"

As if to get Devreux's attention, Scott raised his weapon and let fly with a rip of bullets, perforating the rusting metal of the tractor in the yard. A shard of hot metal hit the gas tank and the tractor detonated with an explosion louder than the thunder that raged in the night sky.

Andrew Scott had moved into the yard in front of the house, oblivious to the driving rain, holding a smoking pistol. He had dragged a bound and gagged Veronica who now knelt in the soaking grass at his feet. He smiled when he saw Luc appear on the porch, and he stroked the side of

Veronica's head with the warm barrel of his gun, parting her blond hair.

"My," he said, "she has such beautiful ears, doesn't she?" He laughed, enjoying his little joke.

Luc's stomach flipped over and he felt a paralyzing fear. It was a shock to see her as Scott's prisoner. Luc dropped the shotgun on the porch and raised his arms, like a POW.

"You want me, Scott. Okay. I'm here. Let the girl go. She's done nothing."

Scott's wild features twisted into an angry frown. "You don't tell me what to do, soldier. I give the orders. You're gonna have to learn that."

Luc came down the steps of the porch toward Scott. "This is between us. She has nothing to do with it."

"She's a fucking gook traitor," Scott snarled. "I gave you an order to kill her and you're going to fulfill that order, Private. Right *here*, right *now!*"

Luc shook his head. He was tired, worn down by the violence and vehemence of his old comrade in arms. When he spoke, his words were almost gentle, soothing.

"Scott, the war's over . . ."

"Not for me," Andrew Scott shot back. "Not for you."

Then his fury overwhelmed him and he lashed out, punching Luc savagely in the head. Veronica whimpered behind her gag and fell away from the terrible flurry of blows. Scott seized Luc's tunic and lifted him, raising him high above his head as if he weighed no more than a doll. He smashed

Luc into the barn door, the old wood splintering under his weight and the force of the throw.

Scott walked toward his prey, strutting his strength and power. "You should have stayed with the platoon," he said with a sneer. "You've grown weak."

He pulled something from the breast pocket of his uniform. It was one of the evil-looking syringes from the Unisol truck, this one filled with the muscle enhancers. Scott jabbed the sharp prong into his chest, draining the cylinder full of liquid into his heart.

Veronica winced as he impaled himself on the needle. As she looked away, she saw out of the corner of her eye the nasty blades of the harrow that sat rusting in the front yard of the farmhouse. The shadow of an idea formed in her head. She fell onto her back and, using her legs, pushed herself across the soaking grass toward the spiky instrument.

Andrew Scott was oblivious to both his victims, reveling in the new power that was pumping through his body. The muscles in his arms and thighs flexed and twitched. Charged with newfound force, he advanced on Luc.

"Now get up and fight," he demanded.

But Luc lay almost lifeless at his feet. He rolled on his side and tried to push himself upright with his arms. The device strapped to his wrist was glowing an ominous yellow, and he could feel the last of his strength draining out of him.

As if he couldn't wait for Luc to stumble to his

feet, Andrew Scott bent down and grabbed him, heaving him a few yards, tossing him into the side of the police car, denting the panel of the passenger door. Luc's head smacked into the glass, cracking it. He slid to the damp ground, bleeding from a gash in the back of his head.

Taking advantage of the mayhem, Veronica had crawled to the harrow unit and hooked the ropes that bound her hands around the sharp steel spikes. She was kneeling with her back to the piece of equipment, working blind. Frantically, she yanked the thick cords over the blade edge, nicking and cutting herself in the process.

Scott was looming over Luc. Devreux stared at him through hazy eyes. "I'm gonna teach you about the chain of command, Private."

He reached down and seized Luc yet again, grabbing his victim by the hair and smashing him into the car, using Luc's skull to deepen the dent already there. He spoke through clenched teeth, head slams punctuating his furious words.

"When I give you an order, you follow it, understand?" He slammed Luc's head against the metal. The door echoed with a dull thud, like a drumbeat.

"When I say jump, you say how high? Got that?" Mercilessly, he beat Luc's head into the side of the car. Luc's eyes were fluttering in his head, like those of a broken doll.

"Learned your lesson?" Scott snarled. "Well, let's see . . ." He grabbed Luc by the collar, dragged him across the lawn and dropped him a few yards from Veronica. Andrew Scott pulled him up into a kneeling position, took a pistol from his belt and thrust it into Luc's hand.

"Now, I give you an order, soldier . . ." Luc's head was dropping, his chin settling on his chest, his eyes closing. Scott yanked his head back by the hair and raised Luc's right hand, steadying the gun, aiming it squarely at Veronica.

The ropes on her wrists were beginning to give, but she froze in her frenzied labors when she saw the gun. Her gag muffled her scream, but her terrified eyes spoke volumes.

"Now," commanded Scott, "let's see you waste that gook traitor."

Luc managed to focus his eyes on the target. "No . . . ," he said groggily. "Please, no . . ."

The blades of the harrow had almost sliced through the ropes. She was almost free.

Scott was speaking softly into Luc's ear. Luc tried to resist, pulling away from his torturer, but he was too weak; Scott held him firmly. The gun never wavered from its target.

"Should we shoot her in the heart? The chest? No. I think we should shoot her in the head. Yeah. The head." His hand closed over Luc's, his finger on the trigger. Veronica looked away, anticipating the bullet.

"Fire!" shouted Scott.

The hammer cocked and smashed back down. There was no roar, no explosion, only the metallic click of a harmless, unloaded weapon.

"Son of a bitch!" screamed Scott, hurling the useless weapon into the night. "Goddammit!"

The harrow blades had cut through the ropes, and Veronica sprung to her feet. Luc saw that she was free and managed to cry out, using the last ounces of his dwindling strength. "Run, Veronica! Run!"

Veronica turned and ran, stumbling in the soggy ground. Scott watched her for a moment, then unclipped a grenade from his belt and heaved it after her.

Luc saw the grenade leave Scott's hand, and he vainly tried to pull himself from the ground. "No! Scott, no!"

Veronica disappeared into the darkness, but the grenade caught her. There was an explosion, a flash of flame and a pall of smoke. It died away in an instant, to be replaced by a long, anguished scream.

It was more than Luc could stand. His hatred and fury overwhelmed his injuries, and suddenly he found himself on his feet. Scott was staring at the site of the explosion and listening to Veronica's dying scream as if it were sweet music. He turned back to Luc just in time to see the sole of Luc's boot, a flying, charging kick, slamming him up against the rotten timbers of the barn. Luc was right on top of him, another savage kick aimed at Scott's head. But Scott's reflexes still had an edge to them. He reached out and got Luc's boot in his grasp, stopping the kick before it could hit home. Luc didn't think—he reacted. Launching himself off the ground he aimed his free leg at Scott, the heavy sole of his boot slamming hard into his enemy's jaw. Both men toppled to the ground.

But Scott was first to his feet. He grabbed at Luc and punched him three times, short hard jabs to the face. Luc's head snapped back so hard it seemed as if his neck would break. But he didn't go down again.

Scott smiled evilly. "Now that's the spirit, soldier," he yelled. But Luc was weakened. Scott grabbed him by the shoulders and threw him into the barn. Luc hit the hard floor violently, sliding a few feet. He lay there a second, the wind knocked out of him. His eyes swept the room and he saw his parents, his eyes growing wide and unbelieving. Tears were coursing down his mother's lined face. His father was deathly pale.

"They're traitors too, Private."

Scott was standing framed in the barn door. He looked eight feet tall.

"Tonight you're all going to die," he said, striding into the barn.

Luc felt weak and powerless, but he was not ready to give up. He staggered to his feet. "Give it your best shot, Scott," he managed to gasp.

Scott swung at Luc, a long hard blow that seemed to come from the floor, all of his weight and strength behind it. Luc dodged the punch and Scott's fist slammed into the wall, poking a hole in the wall of the stall.

Luc summoned up his strength and kicked Scott as hard as he could in the balls, doubling him over. As he toppled, a syringe fell from his flak jacket and Luc grabbed for it—but not fast enough. A stinging back hand from Scott sent him sailing away from the serum, the hypodermic rolling under a stall door. Luc dove for it, reaching into the stall, feeling for the life-giving medicine. His hand scrabbled desperately through the debris and hay on the floor until his fist closed around the glass cylinder.

Without hesitating, he jammed the syringe into his chest and pushed down, shooting all the liquid into him.

"Time to put you to rest," growled Scott, grabbing him from behind, lifting him to his feet. "Say good night, asshole . . ."

He spun Luc around and slammed his fist into his face again and again, sending Luc reeling. Scott moved in for the kill, his bloody fist streaking toward Luc's face for the death blow. The serum coursing through Luc's veins kicked in. His hand shot out and caught Scott's massive fist in mid-arc. His fingers closed like a vise, the bones in Scott's hand and arm cracking.

Luc tossed away the empty syringe. "Good night, asshole. I took my medicine."

A slashing blow blasted Scott backward, throwing him through the stall wall in a shower of splintered wood. Before Scott had a moment to recover from the punishment, Luc kicked out and slammed him into the next stall.

Luc threw himself on his enemy, grabbing him around the waist like a linebacker on a quarterback. The combined force of the two big bodies threw them through another wooden partition. Three savage punches slammed into Scott's face and midsection, sending him reeling. There was the salty taste of blood in his mouth and the flash of something like lightning in his brain—pain.

Scott knew he was fighting for his life. He snatched a length of metal railing off the destroyed stall wall and lashed out with it, missing Luc's head by inches.

Luc grabbed a rusty shovel from the barn floor and blocked the wild blows. The two men stood toe to toe, swinging their crude weapons, sparks exploding as metal hit metal.

Luc may have had new-found strength, but Scott was far from finished. He battled his enemy into a corner of the barn, ready to finish him off if only he could land a decisive blow. Luc, his back to the wall, could only swing wildly. The metal pipe met the shovel and the weapons locked. Scott jerked the pipe hard, snatching the shovel out of Luc's blood-slick hands.

"Now, asshole!" Scott screamed. He raised the shaft of metal high.

Luc's rock hard hand caught the shank and stopped it in mid-blow. Then he twisted and shoved hard, jamming the pipe into Scott's stomach, staggering him.

Luc was starting to realize that his enhanced strength was almost without limits. He nailed Scott again and again with body blow after body blow, piling on, punishing his adversary with all the power he possessed. Scott was doubled over, fear in his eyes now.

Luc grabbed him and threw him against the outside wall of the barn, Scott's heavy body smashing through the weak old timbers. He landed in a heap in the wet grass, his head only inches from the old spiked shredder.

Scott staggered to his feet, ready to face his attacker once again. Luc ran out of the barn and threw himself into the air, his right leg straight out, his boot smacking square into Scott's face. The force of the blow threw him through the air and backward onto the unforgiving spikes of the shredder.

A dozen steel points perforated his body, puncturing him through his back and sticking out of his chest and stomach, arms and thighs. Scott screamed out in pain, staring wide-eyed at the bloody points protruding from his body.

"You son of a bitch!"

Luc stared, both horrified and relieved at what he had done. This *had* to be the end of Scott and his single-minded murderous pursuit. No man, Unisol or not, could come back from a dozen deep wounds.

Then, painfully, slowly, Scott started pulling himself off the spiked barrel of the machinery. First he worked free his left arm, then his right. He curved his upper body forward, pulling himself from the blades that held his chest. Then he worked on his legs, and finally he dragged his punctured stomach off the last of the points. He stood unsteadily on his lacerated legs, his body a bloody mess.

"You motherfucker," he gasped, his eyes boring into Luc's. "You're dead . . ."

Luc smashed back, kicking out at Scott again, slamming him back onto the bloody blades, impaling him anew.

The new wounds seemed to be more than even Andrew Scott could stand. His eyes grew wide in pain and terror, then rolled back up in his skull, his head falling limply.

Luc stood in the driving rain, his chest heaving and falling, staring at Scott's slack form impaled on the spikes. Cautiously, he staggered toward the torn and tortured body of his foe.

He peered into Scott's lifeless eyes and nodded to himself. It was finally over . . .

But it wasn't. Scott's bloody hand reached out and grabbed Luc by the throat and with the last desperate strength in his body started pulling him toward the evil spike that protruded through his chest.

Luc snatched at the hand that had his throat in a death grip, but he couldn't break the grasp. He was being pulled closer and closer, the spike aimed squarely at his eye. Before Scott died, he was determined to kill his sworn foe.

But Luc would not allow it. He would not permit it. The last of his strength surged, pulsing through his veins. He broke Scott's grip then grabbed his arm and snapped it in two—crack!—as if breaking a twig.

Luc reached down and started up the harrow. The drum turned slowly at first, but then, as the engine picked up, it gained speed, the blades of the machine tearing Scott's flesh and sinew into a bloody pulp. The twisting spikes ground into him, stripping an anguished scream from his throat, a long, wild death howl, a shriek of pain and hot hatred, a scream so loud and alive with anger it drowned out Luc's triumphant words.

"I'm alive!" yelled Luc.

Chapter Fifteen

Luc stumbled to the barn and quickly untied his mother and father.

"Are you all right? I'm sorry. I'm sorry you were mixed up in this . . ."

Their hands freed, the Devreux family embraced one another. Mrs. Devreux tried to say something through her tears, but choked on her words.

"Don't worry about us," said Mr. Devreux. "Where is the young woman? Your friend . . ."

"I must find her," said Luke. He stood up and hurried out of the barn, back into the rain.

Luc was drained, exhausted, but he was determined to gather the strength to find Veronica. He staggered toward the still-smoking crater where the grenade had hit and gouged up the earth. His voice fought with the thunder and the rain, his shouts desperate and anguished.

"Veronica! Veronica!" He caught sight of her

lying deathly still on the ground a few feet from the blast site. She looked limp and broken; her clothes were sodden.

Luc rushed to her. He knelt next to her and picked her up. "Veronica?"

Her eyelids fluttered and opened; her eyes looked, unfocused, at his worried face.

"Are you all right?" he asked.

She smiled crookedly. "Boy, do I have a headache . . ."

Relief flooded through him, and he hugged her, embracing her passionately, emotionally. She responded avidly, pressing herself against his bruised, broken and bloody body.

Luc allowed himself a moment of respite, squeezing her tight, forgetting for a second or two the blood and the pain, all the violent death he had witnessed.

Suddenly, Veronica pulled back. "Where's Scott?"

Luc smiled slightly. "He's around." There were pieces of Andrew Scott scattered all over the Devreux front yard.

"How do you feel?"

Luc sensed every bone, joint, muscle and sinew in his body aching. He felt as if he had been hit by a dozen trucks. He was tired and bruised, but alive.

"I feel like a fifty year old," he said.